Praise for
Do You Know
What I'm Not Telling You

Even if you don't live in New York, Karen Wunsch's collection of intimate short stories will make you feel like a native. Wunsch takes to Manhattan streets with the precise eye of an urban archeologist. Whether her characters are in a yoga studio, a coffee shop, or just walking down the street, her prose is vivid and surprising, but never more so than when she writes about relationships and the humor and neurotic baggage that come with them. As one of her characters might say, her stories glisten like Central Park after a rainstorm.

Betsy Carter, author of *We Were Strangers Once*

These are wonderful stories, the kind you can't stop reading, subtle and rich, full of encounters between oddly matched people. They exist in ordinary time, then end in distinctive, timeless, illuminating ways. A world is created, urban, suburban, full of births, deaths and marriages, full of small troubles and big ones, full of life, in short.

Myra Goldberg, author of *Whistling and Other Stories*

There is an effortless quality to Karen Wunsch's stories that belies their careful architecture, a tranquility that belies a deep desire. Her characters move as if through dreams of their own lives, rearranging details here and there, scheming about improvement, all the while sensing that an awakening could come through the next doorway. Her characters yearn too for deeper connection with other lives, are consumed with the ways others promise to complete us.

Peter Grimes, Editor, *Pembroke Magazine*

Karen Wunsch's stories crackle with ambivalent passions and latent sabotage. This chilling debut collection introduces us to a writer who has an almost forensic understanding of human frailty.

Minna Zallman Proctor, Editor, *The Literary Review*

Do You Know What I'm Not Telling You?
and Other Stories

Karen Wunsch

These stories first appeared, in slightly different form, in the following publications:

"Can I Go Now?" *New World Writing*
"What Do You Have to Show Me?" *Crazyhorse*
"Do You Still Love Me?" *Beloit Fiction Journal*
"Little Ghost Face," *The Literary Review*
"Candy Apple Red," *Willow Springs*
"You Owe Me One," *Ascent*
"The One Who Makes You Laugh," *Pembroke Magazine* (forthcoming)
"The Super's Son," *The Literary Review*
"Half-Kidding," *Michigan Quarterly Review*
"Do You Know What I'm Not Telling You?" *Chautauqua*
"Don't Ask Don't Tell," *Ascent*

for Jim

CONTENTS

Do You Know What I'm Not Telling You?

Can I Go Now?

When Ollie came home Friday afternoon Rosie had everything packed, including several bottles of breast milk for four-month-old Amanda. He was finally over the nasty flu that for weeks had kept him from helping much with childcare and household chores. His cough had disrupted Rosie's few hours of sleep, making her cranky, resentful and, worst of all, guilty because of course it wasn't his fault. Now he was taking Amanda to his mother's country house so Rosie could have the weekend off.

When they'd met she was in her thirties, teaching literature at Columbia, and writing a book about Leonard Cohen's novels. She'd finally broken up with her married lover. But although she'd grown up in Manhattan, she'd begun to feel she no longer belonged in this city where everyone seemed eager to get her job, apartment, and seat at Starbucks. Another woman already had the man she wanted to marry. Ollie, naturally pale, with light brown hair and wire-rimmed glasses, was the IT person at a small law firm. He was her age and single, but they didn't have a lot in common—he loved technology and gadgets and rarely read novels. But there was something about the undemanding and uncritical way he loved her that made her feel better about herself, especially after she didn't get tenure.

As Rosie walked them to the car, she couldn't stop looking at Amanda, with her big dark eyes and wispy dark hair. It was Halloween, and she was wearing her orange sweater with ghosts all over it. Until the last minute Rosie wasn't sure she'd be able to let her go.

But by the time she got back to her apartment she was almost giddy at the prospect of two nights of uninterrupted sleep. When the friend she'd planned to have dinner with cancelled, Rosie looked up times for a few movies, then decided to go to a yoga class.

She changed into her exercise clothes, pleased that although her stomach wasn't as flat as it had been, her pants were just a little tight. She liked the way her small breasts were larger now that she was nursing. Standing before the full-length mirror, she pulled her dark hair back into a ponytail, looked into her big dark eyes, and hoped she was as attractive as she had been. On her way to class she kept seeing small children in costumes, and she missed Amanda so much she almost called Ollie to tell him to come home.

The yoga studio was in a brownstone on the Upper West Side. Perhaps because of Halloween, the class wasn't crowded. There were mainly women Rosie's age or younger, plus a young man with a ponytail and a woman with gray hair. Someone had already taken Rosie's favorite spot, by the windowed back door that overlooked a rock garden. The big white high-ceilinged room was bare except for piles of yoga equipment along the walls, but when the lights were dimmed, it seemed almost beautiful. Although many of the students were stretching, Rosie just lay on her mat on her back, her hands at her sides in corpse pose, her eyes open wide so she wouldn't fall asleep. She hoped there wasn't traffic and that Amanda was sleeping and Ollie was okay—he tended to catch whatever flu or virus was going around. When they were first together she'd found this sort of appealing, especially when he was recuperating and she'd come home from work to find him in her bed, propped up against pillows, her flowery duvet half-covering his surprisingly hairy chest. She'd thought that if she were a painter she'd paint his portrait; she'd call it "Ollie in Bed." As she heard the soft, bell-like and tuneless music that Jill, her favorite instructor, always played as she dimmed the studio lights, Rosie tried to empty her mind and concentrate on her breathing, but she kept thinking about how before long, Amanda would be three hours away

Rosie had taken Jill's prenatal class and she appreciated that unlike other teachers, who treated yoga as a series of stretching exercises, Jill—who used to be a lawyer—was at least somewhat spiritual. When at the end of class she'd say, "The light in me salutes the light in you," she'd sound as if she meant it. In her early forties, she was small and skinny, with small pointy breasts and short, grayish-blonde hair. There was a rumor that she was gay. She'd mentioned she was a lapsed Catholic and came from someplace rural in the Midwest. Rosie was Jewish and found it amusing that Jill would talk about schlepping and noshing and kibitzing and always said mazel tov when a new mom would bring in her infant for everyone to ooh and aah over. Rosie wondered if Jill had a Jewish partner.

For the first half of class they lay on their backs in various poses. Although Rosie tried to concentrate, she'd think about things like Ollie, in the rocking chair his mother had put in his old room, giving Amanda a bottle. She hoped he'd be patient about burping her, and that he'd remember to use the ointment for her diaper rash.

Just thinking about Amanda made her breasts leak. Jill came over once to adjust Rosie's position. Her touch was both gentle and firm. If she was aware of the wet spots on Rosie's tee shirt, she gave no indication.

As soon as Jill had them turn onto their stomachs, Rosie realized that her right breast was painful. Even through her tee shirt and bra she could feel that it was hard and warmer than her left one. Her skin prickled and she began to sweat. The other students were on their hands and knees, hunching over and then arching their backs as they moved from cat to cow positions. Rosie sat up.

Jill came right over. "Are you okay?" she asked softly.

"I'm not feeling great." Although she knew that nursing mothers could get infections from clogged milk ducts, she worried it was something more serious. She also worried it wasn't enough of an emergency to call her doctor. If she called Ollie he might come back unnecessarily. She dreaded going back to her empty apartment. "Can I just rest here for a while?"

"Of course."

For the rest of the class Rosie sat on her mat without moving except to occasionally touch her sore breast. It was definitely warmer than the other one and felt hard. She was grateful that the other students, focused on their own bodies, seemed unaware that she was just sitting there.

After the final *oms*, Jill came over to Rosie. "This was the last class of the night, so you're welcome to stay here and call your doctor or husband or maybe rest a little more. I have lots of paperwork I can do."

"I guess I'll call my doctor."

Jill insisted on bringing over her purse. "I'll be out in reception if you need me." She turned up the studio lights and closed the door.

Rosie's doctor wasn't there, but the doctor who called her back said it sounded like mastitis, which wasn't serious, and he'd phone in a prescription for an antibiotic. "Don't stop nursing!"

When Rosie, embarrassed, said that Amanda was away for the weekend, he asked if she had a breast pump.

"I do." She didn't say she hated using it.

"Use it!"

Rosie couldn't decide whether to call Ollie.

Jill came back and asked if everything was okay.

"The doctor said it happens to nursing mothers. He doesn't want me to stop nursing, but Amanda's at my mother-in-law's for the weekend. With my husband."

"Do you have one of those pumps?"

"I do." Her eyes filled with tears. "I feel like I never should have let my family go away."

"Nothing's your fault, Mommy! And it's going to be okay," Jill said softly. "I'll tell you what. Lie down in corpse pose. I'll get some blankets and then I'll lie down too and we'll concentrate on our breathing." She dimmed the lights. "I could use a break."

Rosie knew she should pick up her medicine, pump her breasts and call Ollie. But she lay down again. Turning her head, she could see a sliver of moon above the rock garden.

Jill rolled up two blankets lengthwise and put one under Rosie's neck and the other under her knees. She lay on the floor next to her. "Let's focus on our breath," she said.

Rosie tried to concentrate. She'd never gone so long without nursing, though, and her nipples began to dribble milk again. "Shit!" she muttered. She couldn't believe she'd said shit in the studio. It was like a desecration. She started crying.

"What is it?" Jill sat up.

Rosie pulled up her shirt. She unhooked her nursing bra, her breasts tumbled out, and milk trickled down to her belly.

"My breast is sick," she said, lifting her right breast. "Feel it."

Jill hesitated, then touched it lightly. "It's warm… maybe a little hard."

Rosie saw the breast pump, her dark apartment. "It would help if you sucked it," she whispered. Her heart was pounding. "Please."

Jill, on her knees, had been leaning toward Rosie, but she drew back a little.

"It doesn't taste bad or anything," Rosie said. "It's sort of thin and almost sweet."

Jill didn't move or speak.

"Please. It would be…a mitzvah." Reaching up, Rosie put her hand on Jill's head and gently but firmly pushed it towards her breast.

Jill took Rosie's nipple into her mouth and sucked it gently.

It hurt a little. Rosie closed her eyes.

"Is this okay?" Jill asked.

"It's fine."

When her milk first came in she'd offered Ollie her breast, but he worried about depriving Amanda and barely sucked it.

"Is this okay?" Jill asked again.

"It's fine." Amanda nursed in a more focused way… she would have already emptied it…Rosie almost smiled at the idea of her daughter's efficiency. "I think you got most of it," she said after a while.

Jill sat up—her lips and chin were wet—but Rosie didn't move. Her other breast was dripping milk, and she wanted Jill to suck it too. Occasionally she'd feel aroused when Amanda nursed, but that was nothing like this. Her phone vibrated. Worried it was Ollie and there was a problem with Amanda, Rosie sat up.

It was a text from one of her friends. Rosie put the phone back in her purse.

Jill began folding the blankets.

"I don't know what to say," Rosie murmured. "It seems so stupid to say, Thank you."

"I hope it helped." Jill sounded matter-of-fact, the way she did when students thanked her after class. But her tee shirt had damp spots of milk on it, and Rosie felt a kind of love for her.

Jill insisted on bringing Rosie her jacket and holding it for her to put on. She walked her to the door.

"Thank you." Rosie made a face to show how the words were inadequate.

They hugged briefly—"Be well, Mommy!" —and then Jill went back inside.

By the time Rosie got to the drugstore, she was trembling. Like a lot of her teenage camp friends, she'd had occasional crushes on some of the female counselors— it was part of the camp culture. Before long, though, she began dating boys. Before Ollie, she'd had a lot of boyfriends. Sometimes she worried that she didn't love Ollie as much as she'd loved her married boyfriend, but their sex had always been good, and as soon as she got pregnant she'd felt even more committed to him. Occasionally she'd be drawn to a pretty woman who was dressed up and smelled good and whose femininity was girlier than hers. But she'd never been tempted or come close to having sex with a woman.

By the time Ollie called, Rosie had taken an antibiotic, drunk half a beer, and calmed down.

Telling him about her mastitis, she emphasized that she felt better already. "See you Sunday," she said. If she told him what had happened with Jill, he probably wouldn't be angry or upset, but she was pretty sure he wasn't the type who'd get horny just hearing about it. It would be her little secret.

The next morning, Rosie's phone woke her.

"How are you?" Jill said.

Rosie touched her breast, which was no longer as warm or hard. She realized she'd slept through the night. "Definitely better."

"I'm sort of in your neighborhood," Jill said.

Remembering what had happened in the studio, Rosie hoped Jill hadn't been aware of how aroused she'd been. She wondered if Jill had been excited, too.

"I'd like to stop by," Jill was saying. "I won't stay long."

Rosie told herself that it wasn't as if Jill were some big horny man she'd be letting into her apartment. And she owed her something. "Come on over," she said heartily. Still, she wished that Ollie—or even just Amanda—were there.

She began pumping her breasts. Aside from Ollie, the only people who'd seen her pump had been her mother and a close friend. They'd laughed because the machine not only seemed to be talking, but it said "Tina Fey." But Rosie didn't want to pump in front of Jill.

She'd just finished and was putting on one of Ollie's sweatshirts when her doorbell rang.

"The doorman didn't call up to announce you," Rosie told Jill brightly. "You must look trustworthy." She thought that was a stupid thing to say.

Jill opened her jacket, but said she'd keep it on. She sat on the edge of the sofa. Rosie sat so there was a space between them.

"Can I give you coffee? Or tea?" Jill seemed like the herb-tea type.

Jill didn't want anything.

She was wearing the faded black pants she wore to yoga and a tee shirt. Rosie had a feeling that when Jill was younger she'd been cute-cute, rather than pretty-cute. She was still sort of cute, but Rosie didn't feel attracted to her. She looked at a picture of Amanda on the bookcase, staring solemnly at the camera with her big dark eyes, and her breasts started leaking. She hoped Jill wouldn't notice. She wished Jill would tell her what she wanted, but she just sat there looking uncomfortable.

"I'm wondering if you hate yoga clothing stores like Lululemon as much as I do," Rosie finally said.

"I'm not as much against the commercialization of yoga as you'd think," Jill said. "It gets a lot of people to at least try it."

"So you were a lawyer?"

"I was a lawyer," Jill said lightly. "Everyone told me I'd hate it, and of course they were right. I don't miss the money. I own my apartment and basically just go to cheaper restaurants. I'm much happier now." She blew her nose into a big white handkerchief that reminded Rosie of the ones her father used.

Jill took a deep breath. "I have to tell you that I feel uncomfortable about last night," she said. "What concerns me is that I'm your teacher, and it happened in my place of work."

Rosie was relieved. "I already forgot about it," she said. "Also, it never happened." She smiled.

Jill bit her lip.

"Listen," Rosie said. "I'll put whatever you want in writing. Just tell me what to say. We can go right out and get it notarized." It was hard to believe she was suddenly free to come and go as she pleased.

"Actually, I'm a notary, too," Jill said.

Rosie hesitated. "Also, I can certainly go to another yoga studio."

Jill didn't say anything.

"You'll never see me again," Rosie said. "And I'll never tell anyone. Promise!"

"I believe you." Jill stood up. "I feel better." She zipped up her jacket. "You don't have to go to another studio. And you're welcome in my class any time."

"We'll see," Rosie said. But she decided to try the new Pilates place or join a gym. It was the least she could do.

As soon as Jill left Rosie was about to call the friend who'd texted her in the studio and tell her all about what had happened, but remembering her promise, she went out for a mani-pedi instead.

During the next few weeks Rosie would think of something about that night —like the way she'd pushed

Jill's head toward her breast in the same way a man would push a woman's head toward his penis, or she'd remember the milk stains on Jill's tee shirt, or how she'd said "Shit!" in the studio—and she could almost feel herself blushing. Amanda started to go longer between feedings, and when Ollie got a raise they hired a part-time nanny. One day Rosie went to a movie, another day she had a massage. She and Amanda joined a group of moms and their babies at a nearby Starbucks. Hearing the women complain about their husbands, Rosie felt better about her marriage. Occasionally she'd see a pretty woman all dressed up as if she were going someplace exciting and Rosie would enjoy looking at her, but that would be all.

On a sunny Saturday morning shortly after New Year's, Rosie and Ollie took Amanda for a drive along the Hudson.

In the car Ollie asked Rosie to play Leonard Cohen's "Suzanne." Since she'd been turned down for tenure, his songs could make her feel bad about herself, but now she wanted to move on. As Cohen sang, "And she feeds you tea and oranges/That come all the way from China," for some reason Rosie thought about Jill. She rarely thought about her anymore and mainly felt guilty she hadn't tried a Pilates class or joined a gym.

Amanda woke up, and she seemed to like "Suzanne."

Ollie stopped at a quaint-looking town and suggested they take a walk.

They put Amanda in her stroller and found a small park. Later they ate lunch in a café that had red and white checked tablecloths and dried flowers on the tables. Sipping mulled cider they discussed various summer plans and decided that the easiest thing would be to stay at his mother's country house. Rosie felt lucky they had such a nice place to go to. Breastfeeding Amanda, she thought about how Ollie used to be embarrassed when she nursed in public, but lately he didn't even seem to notice. He was wearing one of the sweatshirts she'd borrow when she first nursed Amanda

He saw Rosie looking at him and smiled almost shyly.

She reached across the table and took his hand.

An older woman sitting a few tables away kept glancing at them. *She thinks we're a happy family.* Rosie remembered how when she'd go out with her married lover, she'd see families she envied.

They took a more direct and less scenic route back to the city. Rosie noticed a mall that had a Best Buy and although she hated malls—she'd count the minutes until she could reasonably ask, "Can we go now?" —she told Ollie he could stop.

"You want me to stop at a Best Buy?" he asked her happily.

After looking at a lot of dishwashers, he ended up with a printer that was on sale. Standing with him on one of the long checkout lines Rosie saw a pretty woman wearing patent leather heels, a dark red coat with a black fur collar and cuffs, and a fur hat with a ribbon in the back. Rosie kept sniffing the flowery perfume she assumed was hers.

"Do you think she's attractive?" she whispered to Ollie.

"Yes."

Rosie laughed.

"What's so funny?"

"Nothing really."

A few days later he woke up with a cough that lingered and kept her up at night even when she slept in another room and turned up her white noise machine. Although he seemed better after a few days, in the middle of sex he had a coughing fit. When it was over he wanted to go back to their lovemaking, but Rosie was no longer in the mood.

He worked all week even though his cough persisted, but as soon as he got home he'd go right to bed.

On Saturday he stayed in bed and Rosie had a tiring day with Amanda, who was getting her first tooth and cranky. In the late afternoon Ollie finally came out of the bedroom. Rosie was surprised he'd shaved and was dressed.

"I'm better. Why don't you get out and do something for yourself?" He took Amanda from her arms. "Get a pedicure. Go to yoga or something."

Amanda started crying.

"Maybe I should stay…."

"Go!"

She looked at the clock. Jill must be teaching her last class of the day. She was the only other person who knew what had happened that night, and Rosie suddenly wondered if they could be friends.

She was walking toward the studio when Jill came out. She wore a pea jacket and a dark knitted hat.

"If you hurry you can still make Mark's class," Jill told her.

"That's not why I'm here."

"Oh?"

"Are you free? Maybe we can get coffee."

"Now?"

"I thought maybe we could talk."

Jill bit her lip. "Let's go to my apartment," she said. "It's not too far."

She lived in a one-bedroom in an anonymous-looking high-rise. Although her furniture was nondescript, a big chandelier shaped like a hot air balloon hung in the small entryway.

They sat in the sparsely furnished living room. Jill wore a tee shirt and faded yoga pants. Rosie looked down at her sweater that wasn't tight any more. She only nursed Amanda at bedtime now. She wondered if Jill noticed how much smaller her breasts were.

"I love your chandelier," she said. She was tempted to ask where she'd bought it, but she didn't want to have that kind of conversation.

"It was Annie's," Jill said. "My ex's." Jill got her phone and showed Rosie a picture of a woman in her thirties with freckles and a lot of auburn hair.

"She lives in Brooklyn now. With the woman she left me for."

"That must be hard."

"In a few months they're going to have a baby."

Rosie didn't ask which woman was pregnant. "That must be really hard."

Jill shrugged. "It's easier than it was." She smiled brightly. "I don't know about you, but I'm hungry. How about some soup?"

"Soup would be great."

"I need to go shopping, but I'll see what I can do."

She didn't want any help. Rosie got up and looked at the bookcase. There weren't many novels. Rosie texted Ollie that she was having dinner with Jill, then texted again that Jill was her yoga teacher. She felt sad she wouldn't be putting Amanda to bed.

Jill brought out mugs of what looked like tomato soup, and a basket of rice crackers. "It's an improvised soup. I only had V8 juice, the kind without salt? But I added some shredded carrots, and it's not bad. I can give you salt, if you want."

It was bland and watery, but Rosie didn't ask for salt. "Do you have any wine?"

"I stopped drinking when I stopped practicing law, but I'll look."

She came back with a bottle of Manischewitz and made a wry face. "Sorry. This is all I've got."

Rosie laughed. "I haven't had Manischewitz Concord Wine since the Seders of my childhood."

"Annie was Jewish, but we broke up before what would have been my first Seder."

"Maybe I'll just have water," Rosie said. "Actually, I'll have the wine."

It was as sickeningly sweet as she remembered.

She was about to complain about the commercialization of yoga when she had a vague memory of bringing it up when Jill came to her apartment. She finished her wine, poured herself more, and alternated a sip of soup with two sips of wine. Dunking a rice cracker in the soup didn't help. She decided it was the worst meal she'd ever had.

"Why did you want to see me?" Jill asked.

No longer feeling they could be friends, Rosie stood up. "Let's go to the living room." Although she hadn't quite finished her soup, she started to clear.

"Leave the dishes," Jill said.

Rosie sat on one end of the sofa; Jill sat on the other.

Not sure what to say, Rosie talked about Leonard Cohen's novels.

"I thought he only wrote songs," Jill said.

"Do you like his songs?"

"I don't know a lot of them."

"Do you like 'Suzanne'? The one about the tea and oranges?"

"What do you want to talk to me about?"

Rosie looked at Jill's tee shirt, then looked away. She had to say something. "Sometimes I think about that night in the studio."

"And?"

Rosie tried to focus on her breathing. "For one thing, I wish I hadn't said shit."

"I don't remember that."

Rosie was sorry she'd come. What had she been thinking? "That night…did you swallow it? Or spit it out?" She hadn't planned to ask. It was the kind of thing a man might want to know.

Jill looked relieved. "Your milk?" She smiled. "I can't say for certain…maybe a little of both? It was thin, and almost sweet."

Rosie decided not to ask if it had felt like a kind of love.

She left soon afterward, and when she got home Ollie was sitting up in bed, reading a magazine. He coughed.

"Are you okay?" she asked him.

"I'm fine." He put down his magazine.

She could feel the wine. "How was Amanda?"

"Amanda's fine. Her rash is almost gone."

Usually Rosie would want to hear all the details about what he and Amanda had done, but something was bothering her. Ollie in bed. Again. She told herself to forget it. She told herself not to look for trouble.

"It's probably a good thing we're going to your mom's this summer," she said.

"I guess."

"I mean, if you get sick, we won't have to cancel any plane or hotel reservations."

"I'll be fine," he said mildly.

She told herself to stop. "Well, you don't have a very good track record."

"I'll be fine," he said firmly. He picked up the magazine. "How was your dinner with your teacher?"

Rosie took off her sweater. "It was the worst meal I ever had."

"That's too bad."

"Did I tell you that Jill is gay?"

He was flipping through the magazine. "That's nice."

As she sometimes did, Rosie undressed in stages, putting on her nightgown before taking off her jeans and boots. Although Ollie rarely criticized her appearance, for some reason this always seemed to annoy him.

"Are you coming or going?" he'd say.

"Are you coming or going?" he asked her.

"I'm not sure," she said softly.

"What?"

"Nothing."

"Good night." He turned off his light.

In the dark, she took off the rest of her clothes. And then right before getting into bed, she took off her nightgown, too.

What Do You Have to Show Me?

Simon was drawn to Pippa's dating profile because she was pretty—dark eyes and long brown hair with bangs—and her name sounded like she'd be good in bed. Thirty-four, a year older than Simon, she described herself as a part-time English professor and full-time poet. Googling her he found her poem, "Hannah and Otto," in a journal. He hoped it would be erotic, but there was a dwarf and a teal blue calf, and he had no idea what was going on. But he was a dermatologist and didn't read a lot of poetry. He also found Pippa's Rate Your Professor profile. Her students said she was an easy grader, and although Simon knew this had nothing to do with sex, he was hopeful.

She suggested they meet in the late afternoon at a Starbucks near her apartment. When he saw her, at a table full of books and papers, wearing a jersey shirt that showed her breasts were small but full, she was prettier than her picture. He couldn't tell what she thought of him. His dark curly hair was receding and he could have lost ten pounds. On the other hand, women liked his blue eyes and were impressed that he was a doctor.

As Pippa cleared her things off the table, he noticed how almost everyone around them, most on computers or phones, looked like they'd been there all day. The whole place seemed worn and tired and not very clean. Although over the years he'd bought coffee at various Starbucks, he couldn't remember ever sitting down in one. This one, on the far East Side of Manhattan, was particularly depressing.

"Should I get us coffee?" he asked Pippa.

"I'm sort of drowning in tea, but get yourself something."

There was a long line. "Actually, I'm okay."

At the table next to them a man Simon's age was being interviewed for some kind of job by a young woman whose arms were covered with tattoos. When Simon occasionally interviewed someone for his small office staff, it was in the spacious midtown office he'd inherited from his father, also a dermatologist. Simon would be behind his big mahogany desk, and the candidate would be across from him in an armchair.

"So what kind of poetry do you write?" He wasn't going to bring up "Hannah and Otto."

Pippa blew her bangs off her forehead. "Personal?"

He suspected she was looking for someone artistic.

He wanted someone he vaguely thought of as more exciting than Kathy, who he'd decided was too conventional. He'd recently broken up with her after almost a year because the next step would have been for them to live together. He'd had enough therapy to be aware he was rebelling against his own conventionality: he'd been a top student who still thought of certain words as SAT words and of nights before a workday as "school nights"; after briefly considering a gap year after college to travel and consider his options, he'd gone right to medical school and then chose his father's profession. He also wanted to sleep with more women, although not necessarily a lot more, before he got married.

"What's the one thing you like best about being a dermatologist?" Pippa asked him.

Although many women would be eager to hear about Botox and SPFs in sunscreen, she didn't seem like the type.

He talked about helping adolescents with acne, adding that he was thinking about giving up cosmetic procedures.

She nodded approvingly.

"So you teach college?" he asked her.

"Two classes. I'm mainly a poet."

He wondered what she lived on.

They talked about online dating. She hadn't done it much either.

"You were one of the few men who didn't say he likes trying new restaurants and going to the movies. And then they add, 'But I also like to stay in with Netflix and a bottle of red.'"

He laughed, although he liked all those things too.

He'd talked about biking.

"Do you bike?" he asked Pippa.

"Not really."

He shrugged. "Actually, I hurt my knee, so I'm taking a break."

He couldn't think of anything else to say and, apparently, neither could she.

Several people coming and going said Hi or Bye to her.

"You're like the mayor here," he told her.

"I try to come every day."

He felt sort of sorry for her.

He excused himself to go to the bathroom. There was a long line and he didn't feel like waiting.

Back at the table, Pippa was just staring into space. Was she composing a poem?

"I can't believe there's only one bathroom," he said. "Is that even legal?"

She laughed.

He hadn't meant to be funny.

"I should be going," he said. He wished he could go for a bike ride.

"Actually, can I ask you something?" Pippa blew her bangs off her forehead. "This is probably crazy, but are you doing anything tonight?"

"No," he said slowly.

"It would be kind of a favor."

He just looked at her.

"Today's my mom's birthday, and she's coming in from New Jersey and we're going out to dinner. This is sort of wild, but if you came—you wouldn't have to pretend you're a serious boyfriend or anything like that— just seeing me with a doctor would be like the best present I could give her."

Simon wondered if he should be insulted that she was asking him to have dinner with her mother.

"And if you're there she won't talk about things like how she'll pay for me to get my eggs frozen before it's too late."

Simon was pleased that unlike Kathy, Pippa apparently wasn't worried about her biological clock.

"Anyway," she said, "I totally understand if you don't want to do it."

He almost made up an excuse. But it was probably a good restaurant, and Pippa would be grateful, and maybe they'd end up in bed.

✦ ✦ ✦

As soon as he got to the restaurant he saw a woman in her sixties sitting alone. She resembled Pippa around the eyes and mouth and wasn't unattractive, with grey-blonde hair, blue eye shadow, and a bright blue dress. He didn't see Pippa.

"You're Pippa's mom?"

"Is something wrong? Did something happen to Pippa? Tell me what happened."

He was annoyed that Pippa hadn't told her he was coming. "Everything's fine. I'm a friend of Pippa's. Sort of a new friend."

Giving him a big smile, she said, "I'm Marjory," and gestured for him to sit down.

He'd give Pippa five minutes and then find an excuse to leave.

Marjory said she was a psychotherapist.

He had a feeling she'd have a warm, supportive manner.

After he said he was a dermatologist, they talked about Botox and sunscreen.

"One more question," Marjory said. "When my dermatologist comes into the exam room, he always asks, 'What do you have to show me?' It's sort of funny when you think about it, like when we used to have Show and Tell in school." She gave him another big smile. "I was wondering if you say anything similar to your patients."

"That's funny, because my dad was a dermatologist and he'd say the exact same thing. And I guess I say it too." He was moved to think about his father, who'd died several years before.

Pippa was there. "Sorry. The subway was a shit show."

She looked mainly at Simon.

Her dark coat seemed big on her and when she took it off she was wearing a sleeveless dress although it was November. There wasn't a lot of cleavage, but she looked sexier than she had in Starbucks.

As she went on about the subway, she barely looked at Marjory. He hoped he wasn't in the middle of some mother-daughter…what his dad would call a mishegas.

Pippa ordered wine, drank it quickly, ordered more and, when their food came, pretty much stopped talking. He felt like telling her that Marjory was a nice lady and had a job that helped people and probably gave her a good income—Pippa could learn a few things from her.

Marjory was talking about a play starring Matthew Broderick, who was married to Sarah Jessica Parker, who was somehow related to her and Pippa.

"Now she's going to ask if you have any idea how short Sarah Jessica Parker is," Pippa said to him.

He wanted to tell her to grow up. He couldn't re-member ever being so annoyed with someone he barely knew.

Marjory mentioned other movie stars who were short, like Tom Cruise and Daniel Radcliffe.

"Daniel Radcliffe was Harry Potter, right?" Simon said to Pippa.

"Right," she said. "I've heard him on podcasts. He's pretty smart."

"I rarely listen to podcasts," he said.

He thought the food wasn't worth the money, but it was pretty good. He'd get through the rest of the evening and then come back with a woman who'd be more grown-up than Pippa.

When Pippa went to the bathroom Simon tried to be subtle about checking his watch.

Lowering her voice, Marjory told him how Pippa's dad had died when she was five. "She adored him."

Simon wanted to say that was no excuse for spoiling her mother's birthday.

Marjory finished her wine and poured herself more. Simon couldn't decide whether to have another glass—it was a school night.

"I probably had too much to drink," Marjory said, "but can I tell you something else?" She leaned toward Simon. "Pippa can be moody, but she's really a wonderful person. Can I tell you something else?"

Pippa was back.

She blew her bangs off her forehead. "What are you two talking about?"

"Not you," Marjory said.

They talked about the food and the weather. There were a lot of silences. Pippa didn't want dessert. Simon was going to order something for Marjory's sake, but she quickly said she didn't want anything either. Simon let her pay for him.

Saying goodbye to her, Pippa burst into tears. "Sorry, Mom. I'm having a miserable time with this new poem. I know it's no excuse. I love you. Happy Birthday."

Marjory seemed happy enough, but Simon agreed that having trouble writing a poem was no excuse. He'd take Pippa home, and that would be that.

In the Uber Pippa turned to him. "I owe you an apology too. You were great. I could tell she was having a good time. In spite of me."

Simon shrugged.

When they got to her building, a run-down looking brownstone on the far Upper East Side, she said, "Do you want to come up?"

Inside her small studio, she didn't even turn on the light but started taking off her clothes.

Their sex was the first he'd had since Kathy. Pippa seemed to enjoy it too. When he came back from the bathroom afterward—the door wouldn't close unless he first raised the toilet seat—she'd turned on the light and was sitting cross-legged on her bed with a clipboard on her lap.

"I got so involved with my poem, I didn't grade all the papers I have to give back tomorrow." She had a small blanket around her shoulders—her apartment was chilly.

"Do you want me to go?"

"Do you want to go?"

He thought about it. "I want to stay."

Usually he'd pick her up at Starbucks. If she'd had a good day, which mainly depended on whatever poem she was writing, she'd be interested in whatever he talked about, give him flirty smiles and, taking off her boot, move her foot slowly up his leg. When they left, she'd wear her backpack and he'd carry her canvas tote bag, heavy with books and papers. Often she'd stop at CVS, a drugstore chain he disliked. The one she went to was dingy and under-stocked and he was surprised by how, on many items, the small independent drugstore he went to was cheaper.

Although his apartment was much bigger and in a better neighborhood, Pippa preferred hers because her books were there. She'd stop at the fruit and vegetable cart on her corner and buy something. She didn't cook. When they ate out he'd be pleased that unlike Kathy, Pippa didn't order only a salad.

Her apartment was often chilly. Her kitchen was tiny, and one of the few cabinets was blocked by the fridge and couldn't be used. There was no bathtub. None of this seemed to bother Pippa. Apparently writing poetry made everything else in her life all right.

He envied her.

"I like my work, but sometimes I feel stuck," he told her one day.

"Is it as if you're waiting for, say, a local subway, but an express comes and you take it for a few stops. But then you have to wait again for the same local. And when it finally comes, you wonder what you actually accomplished?"

"I guess so." He was intrigued by the way she looked at things.

"I know this is really stupid," he told her, "but when I bike I stop at Stop signs even if no one's crossing."

She took his hand and kissed it.

She rarely talked about her job, for which she had to travel to one community college in Queens and then to another in the Bronx. She was badly paid, few of her students were English majors, and every semester she wouldn't find out until the last minute if there was enough enrollment for her to have a course.

"Is that even legal?" Simon asked her.

She laughed. "Actually, the long subway rides give me extra time to write."

He wasn't surprised to learn she supplemented her income with interest from a trust fund.

He liked it that she was so different from the other

women he'd dated. She exercised only sporadically and didn't drink diet Coke. She'd had a long affair with one of her college teachers who was married but had made her want to be a poet. One night when Simon and Pippa were talking about nothing in particular and she suddenly took a deep breath and blew her bangs off her forehead, he imagined that one day, they'd have a dark-haired child with bangs.

"Sometimes I worry about what you see in me," he told her shyly.

"For starters, my mom really liked you!"

This became their little joke.

After two months he nervously asked if she'd agree to take a break from online dating. She said she'd already done it.

Sitting cross-legged on her sofa, with the small blanket around her shoulders, she started reading poetry to him. She favored women like Sylvia Plath and Anne Sexton, who he secretly thought of as whiney. Another problem was that once Pippa started reading him one poem, she'd come across another and say, "You have to hear this!" That would lead to another, and sometimes she'd go on and on until they'd be too exhausted to have sex.

The poem he liked best was about eating a plum. It was short and kind of sexy and the writer, William Carlos Williams, was also a physician.

"See," Pippa said happily. "You do like poetry."

Although he'd occasionally worry she'd bring up "Hannah and Otto," she never read him her own poems.

When he'd get to Starbucks and she'd be just sitting there looking miserable, he'd know she'd failed to salvage a bad writing day. He'd ask if he should go. She'd say yes, no, maybe, I don't know. She wouldn't want more tea. He'd have coffee—he got to like having caffeine at the end of his workday—and try to concentrate on one of his medical journals. He began to recognize baristas and steady customers. Once he saw one of his patients on the bathroom line.

Pippa would stare into space, occasionally sighing or blowing her bangs off her forehead. When he'd eventually ask what she wanted to do about dinner, she'd say she didn't care. He'd suggest various restaurants. She wouldn't be in the mood for anything. Her fridge had little besides fruit and vegetables, often rotting. Once he left work early to shop for groceries and he made them dinner. It was hard to work in her small kitchen, and everything was under or overcooked. Pippa ate absentmindedly and said it was fine.

Sometimes she'd say, "Maybe fucking will help."

It rarely did.

They didn't fight, but small things, like the sound of her podcasts, began to annoy him. He'd rarely have heard of any of the people being interviewed, and he'd find the drone of their voices going on and on about themselves unpleasant. Although Pippa wasn't as critical of him as his other girlfriends had been, he wondered if she was so involved with her poetry, she just didn't care as much.

One of the few times she was annoyed with him was when he took her to the small independent drugstore near his apartment so she'd see for herself how much nicer—and cheaper—it was than CVS.

"But I don't mind overpaying," she said.

Mainly she suffered over her poetry.

He'd tell himself that whatever was getting to feel stale about his job, it was way better than being a poet.

One night she called him—usually she texted—crying so hard he thought it was some medical emergency. Finally he understood that she was discouraged because her poems kept getting rejected.

He said he'd be right over.

In the Uber he reread "Hannah and Otto." He still couldn't understand it.

When he got to her apartment she'd stopped crying. She asked if he wanted to read her poetry, and handed him a folder.

Even the titles, like "Limnal Dreams," "Terra Cotta Clown," "Ellipsis #9," were discouraging. And even when a line seemed to make sense (although sometimes, for reasons he didn't understand, these lines were in quotes), he couldn't see how it connected with whatever came before or after. He tried to reread a few of the most confusing poems; almost immediately he'd stop concentrating. In the end he had no idea what even one poem was about.

Pippa had been marking papers in her bedroom while he read in the living room. She came in as soon as he finished.

"You hate them!"

He made a fumbling speech about how he wasn't her ideal reader.

"I only ever got one poem published." She started crying again.

"Can I ask you something?" he said. "When you get a poem published, do they pay you, like, by the word?"

She smiled. "Most journals don't pay. A lot of them make you pay to submit to them."

"Is that legal?"

She laughed. After a while she rinsed her face and found two clementines that weren't rotting.

As they ate them she cheered up.

He was frustrated he didn't have the ability to help make her poems at least clearer.

Shortly after what Simon thought of as the poetry crisis, his friend Adam, an anesthesiologist, suggested they meet for dinner at a popular steak house. When Simon saw him waiting at the bar—Adam was gangly and, especially in his baseball cap, boyish looking—he had an impulse to give him a hug, but he just said, Hey. They hadn't seen each other since Simon met Pippa.

The restaurant was crowded and they were seated near a large, noisy table of young men who looked like finance types. Adam showed him pictures of his new baby. Simon showed him Pippa.

"Cute!" Adam said.

"She's a poet."

"That's something different."

They drank whiskey, ate big steaks, and talked about work and a few doctors they both knew.

Simon wanted to tell him how sometimes he worried Pippa was what his dad would call a little meshuga about her poetry.

"I'll tell you one thing," he said. "It's really hard to get poetry published."

Adam belched.

"I don't know how to say this," Simon said—he'd had

more to drink than usual and he wasn't used to eating so much—"but sometimes, with Pippa, I wish…this is going to sound really weird."

"Shoot."

"You know how Pippa has bangs? You saw her picture."

"Pippa has bangs."

Simon wished he'd never said anything. "This is crazy, but sometimes she blows her bangs out of her eyes, and there's this moment when her forehead is…bare. And, this sounds really stupid, but sometimes I wish I could 'freeze' that moment. It's like…a moment in time? You don't know what I'm talking about. It's not your fault."

"You don't like Pippa's bangs?"

Simon pictured Pippa's face. "They're fine. Her bangs are fine. They're her bangs. I'm not even sure what I mean."

"You know what?" Adam was slurring his words. "You sound like a poet."

Simon was embarrassed and vaguely flattered.

It was April and Pippa's birthday, and Simon would be taking her to a trendy restaurant. He'd pick her up at her apartment and she'd be wearing a black dress he hadn't seen, but she promised was sexy. He'd had a great time at a lingerie shop looking at nightgowns. Although he found a short filmy one he really liked, he worried it would be more for him than for her. That morning he got to work early so he could catch up on paperwork and go out later to shop.

He enjoyed being at his office when no one else was there. The wood-paneled rooms had high ceilings and casement windows that got afternoon sun. There was a kitchen and a still-functioning water cooler his father had been proud of; Simon made sure it was always filled. He still wore his father's lab coats, cut more generously than the kind that was currently available. He was sad to be down to his last few.

It was an unremarkable morning. He identified a Lyme disease rash. An older, elegantly dressed woman had what he was pretty sure were bedbug bites. He did cryosurgery on a screaming child's warts. Following his father's rule that if he hesitated about something even briefly during an exam, that meant he should send the patient to a specialist, he told a new patient to get his thyroid checked. Passing the kitchen, he saw his assistant and his receptionist, both older women, drinking coffee and chatting. They were cheerful and friendly, but he suspected they found him awkward. Kathy had stopped by once, and he'd been pleased they could see how attractive and stylish she was. He wondered what they'd think of Pippa.

At noon he went out, bought a hotdog on the street and window-shopped as he ate it. In the window of an antique store he saw a big black shawl draped over an old-fashioned-looking steamer trunk. The shawl was embroidered with a bouquet of scarlet flowers loosely tied with a green velvet ribbon. There was a silky-looking black fringe all around that reminded him of Pippa's bangs. He found the shawl a little granny-like, but he was pretty sure Pippa would like it.

At first the saleswoman wasn't sure it was for sale. She called someone to find out, and it turned out to cost a lot more than he'd planned on spending. But maybe one dull night Pippa would tell him to close his eyes, and when he opened them she'd have the shawl wrapped around her naked body. Very slowly she'd take it off. She'd touch the fringe to her nipples and then, taking out his penis, she'd slowly move the silky strands up and down, barely touching the skin.

For all that to happen, though, he'd have to wait for her to have a good writing day, or for a magazine to publish one of her unreadable poems. What she'd probably do was wrap the shawl around her shoulders as she sat cross-legged on the couch in a tee shirt and sweat pants. She'd be hunched over a clipboard or staring miserably into space. Of course he could buy her the sexy nightgown, too. But he liked the idea of having to choose: it seemed symbolic or metaphorical or something interesting that never would have occurred to him if he hadn't known Pippa.

Do You Still Love Me?

When Nina wanted to change the time for her daughter Emma's pre-school interview, the secretary told her flatly that rescheduling wasn't an option. She didn't have to add that many families would be eager to take their place. Although Nina's husband Steve, an orthodontist, had said he could shift his appointments, Nina—even though she had no appointments—was still indignant. "I can't believe they didn't give us a choice," she complained to Steve that night. In the small town in upstate New York where she'd grown up she'd gone to the local nursery school in a church basement. Steve, who'd always lived in Manhattan, shrugged as if to say, "What can you do?"

They'd put Emma to bed. Nina was lying on the sofa; Steve sat at the other end, trying to read a magazine. Her bare feet were in his lap.

"I'll tell you one thing," she muttered. "If I get an audition I'm really not sure what I'll do...." She knew, and she knew he knew, that she'd go to the interview. Running her fingers through her auburn curls, which Steve called Botticelli rotini, she hoped that he wouldn't point out that she hadn't had an audition—she was an aspiring cabaret singer—for months.

He took off his glasses and rubbed the sore-looking indentations they left on the sides of his nose. "Take it easy. Two years from now we'll be worrying about kindergarten."

"I can't even think about that now."

Since they'd begun the application process she'd had trouble sleeping, and the next day she'd be tired and irritable. He'd tell her, "Pessimists aren't right any more than optimists. Keep track."

She'd mean to do it, but kept forgetting.

Sometimes he'd murmur, "It's only a life!"

Sometimes she found this comforting.

He put down his magazine and began to massage her feet.

"I never thought I'd be this way," she told him. "I mean, I wasn't like this about getting into college."

He sighed.

"How can you not be worried too?"

"I feel everything that you feel," he kissed the top of one foot. "Only not as often. Or as intensely."

She smiled, then frowned. "You don't know the stories I hear. This one mom, after her child's interview—I forget where, he was older—she could see that he'd misspelled his name or something like that, and she knew he wasn't going to get in. Of course she didn't say a word to him and she tried to be cheerful, but as soon as they got outside he said, 'Mommy, do you still love me?'"

Steve picked up his magazine. "Enough with the horror stories!"

The night before the interview, his parents came for dinner. When Nina first knew them she'd wondered if she'd come to feel as if they were her parents, too, because her father died before she was two, and she wasn't particularly close to her mother. Although it hadn't happened, she was usually happy to see Ellen, a college guidance counselor, and Fred, a tax lawyer who didn't say much but was kind. Tonight, though, she wished she and Steve could have had a quiet evening together.

Ellen had insisted on bringing all the food. "You poor kids have enough to do with all the child care!" She always said this as if, Nina thought, being a parent was somehow heroic.

They gave Emma a brightly colored toy xylophone that used to be Steve's. She began playing it right away.

"I love that serious look she gets when she concentrates," Ellen whispered.

Nina loved it, too.

As usual, she appreciated the way Ellen looked: the subtle blonde highlights, her silky ivory-colored blouse sprinkled with violets that seemed to have been scattered here and there.

As Steve described how Emma's interview would be some kind of playdate involving other children who were also applying, he joked about how if he were young now, he wouldn't be able to get into the prestigious high school he'd gone to in the 1990's.

Nina used to enjoy the joke, but suddenly she found it irritating. She wondered if she was getting her period—she had that old feeling, as if she were in a too-warm room but couldn't take off her sweater.

For a while they all watched Emma, who cocked her head as she listened intently to each different sound from the xylophone. Nina couldn't help it: she hoped Emma would be alert like that for the interview. Steve and his parents began reminiscing about the "old New York," a favorite topic.

They liked to argue about old Manhattan telephone

exchanges like BUtterfield 8.

"It was LEhigh 4!"

"You're thinking of LYceum 4!"

They complained about the new, gentrified New York.

"I know there's a lot of banks and chain stores," Nina wanted to say, "but this New York is all I have!" When she was ten she'd visited for the first time, with a friend whose grandmother lived in Manhattan. They'd done lots of touristy things, but what really impressed Nina was the Saturday night the grandmother, before going to bed, gave the girls money and told them they could call a nearby diner that would deliver milkshakes. Standing shyly behind her friend as she tipped the delivery boy, Nina had vowed that one day she'd live in the city. In college she'd worked to save money so that after graduation she could move to Manhattan. And even now, especially at dusk, the city still seemed romantic. Recently when she'd been obsessing about pre-schools, and Steve said they could always move to the suburbs, she'd burst into tears.

Emma climbed on Nina's lap. Clearly tired, she put her head on Nina's shoulder.

"It was LYceum 5!"

Nina was happy to excuse herself to put Emma to bed.

She closed the blinds and dimmed the light, and the small room, with its flowered wallpaper and antique dresser from Steve's old bedroom, seemed cozy. She put Emma on her lap and they rocked in the rocking chair where someone famous Ellen had gone to school with once rocked Steve.

"Can Mommy sing you a lullaby?"

"No singing!"

The one thing Nina found disappointing about Emma was that she didn't like her to sing. When Emma was younger she'd cry; recently she'd occasionally seem interested, but at some point she'd put her small hand over Nina's mouth.

As she settled Emma down and tiptoed out, Nina couldn't imagine how anyone could resist her.

In the dining room Ellen was bringing out many containers of Chinese food from a restaurant that was famous for the number of orders they delivered to Jews on Christmas. She wouldn't let Nina help.

As they ate, Ellen annoyed her by bringing up—again—how she couldn't wait until Nina and Steve moved to a building with a "regular"—theirs was part-time—doorman.

"Actually," Nina felt like saying, "I wish we had no doorman." She was embarrassed when he rushed to take her packages; sometimes she walked around the block so she could get her own cab.

Steve would tell her that doormen had a good union and it was considered a desirable job, but now he gave her a look to show he knew what she was thinking.

She appreciated it.

He and his dad talked about the Yankees. They had the same light brown hair, Fred's receding now. Ellen talked about a movie that the New Yorker critic had loved. Feeling very full—that was definitely the best Chinese food she'd ever had—Nina tried not to yawn.

At one point Ellen put her hand on Fred's arm and left it there.

At first Nina had been embarrassed by the way they'd

be affectionate in public. She wondered what she and Steve would be like after they'd been married as long.

Ellen turned to Fred. "We're going to help clean up and then we're out of here. These poor kids have a big day tomorrow."

As Nina and Steve undressed without speaking—he was wearing the boxers from Switzerland his parents had given him one Chanukah—she remembered how when she'd first moved in with him, he'd been so excited to have her there that as soon as he'd hear her key in the lock he'd rush to open the door. One night he proudly came to bed doused in her perfume. (She'd gently explained that to her, this wasn't sexy.) She loved him, but when he proposed after just a few months, she wasn't as sure: she wanted to focus on improving what she called her "non-career," which consisted mainly of last minute subbing at cocktail lounges in second-rate hotels in New Jersey and Connecticut. Most of the time she did office work for various temp agencies.

"Let's live together for a while and see what happens," she told Steve, but he'd never been madly in love before and said he couldn't wait.

She was also thirty—he was thirty-five—and they wanted to have a child.

She put on a filmy nightgown with a satin ribbon that tied under her breasts.

"I meant to tell you," she said, "some kid in the playground got ringworm and they think it could be from the sandbox!"

He'd taken off his socks and was throwing them, one at a time, into the hamper. One made it.

He came over and tried to put his arms around her. She stiffened. "Tomorrow's the interview."

"So?"

"I'm not in the mood. Sorry."

"How did you learn to make yourself so rigid?" he teased. "Did they teach you that in girls' school?' He tried to untie the ribbon under her breasts.

Moving away, she said, "I didn't go to girls' school." She was tempted to add, "I'm not a rich girl from Manhattan."

When they got into bed, he said, "You smell good," and turned towards her.

"I can't."

"You let things get to you. It's like you have no immune system."

She knew he was right, but didn't want to give him the satisfaction of telling him. "Fuck you!" She wished it hadn't popped out; he never cursed.

He turned to face the wall.

"I'm sorry."

"Do you hear yourself?"

Whenever he said that—and he'd been saying it more often lately—she'd see herself, in one of the slip-like dresses she'd wear when she sang in a club: pushing out her chest and shaking her curls so her sparkly barrette would catch the light, in her soft, breathy voice she'd sing songs like "Send in the Clowns." Suddenly, she was depressed. "Steve?"

He was sleeping.

"Do you still love me?" she whispered.

The preschool was in a nondescript brownstone on the Upper West Side. Nina wore her black jersey top that wasn't as clingy as her other tops and her black skirt that was longer and looser than her other skirts. There were four other couples in the ordinary-looking waiting room, a woman who didn't seem to have a partner, and six children, two of whom were twins. The children were relatively quiet, as if they sensed their parents' tension. To calm herself Nina tried the deep breathing she'd learned in childbirth classes. The woman without a partner kept biting a cuticle. Nina smiled at her and she feebly smiled back. Nina was grateful Steve was with her. He'd not only grown up in this world, but he had a friendly manner that made people comfortable right away. Although men found Nina attractive, she felt that women were wary at first, perhaps because of her sexy clothes. Emma's bright green hair ribbon was coming undone, but when Nina tried to fix it she shook her head.

The director—"Call me Julie!"—came to take them to the playroom. Not fat but on the heavy side, she had a gray wispy bun and wore a long paisley skirt. She explained that the children would be encouraged to go to the play area and parents were to sit in the back of the room.

"But if your child won't let you go," she said, "not to worry!"

One woman waved her hand frantically, then talked about her son's allergies. Nina tried not to dislike her.

There were two young and pretty teachers, and Emma let one of them lead her to a table filled with art supplies. When a boy cried until his mother sat next to him at the small table, Nina avoided looking at them, the way she didn't look at highway accidents or people collapsed on the sidewalk. She also tried not to watch Emma, enthusiastically finger-painting. Steve kept surreptitiously checking his phone.

When the time was up, Julie reminded the parents that "letters" would go out in March.

Families started to leave. Noticing that the mom who'd talked about her son's allergies had stayed behind, Nina was tempted to stay, too, and try to ingratiate herself with Julie or the teachers. She was sure that Steve wouldn't go along with it.

"Was it fun?" they asked Emma when they got outside.

Running ahead of them and then running back, she didn't answer, but she seemed happy enough.

"See," Steve said to Nina as he looked for a cab. "Pessimists aren't always right."

"I admit it wasn't as bad as I thought," Nina said. "I just hope our interview is okay." She bit her lip. "Plus all the other interviews…."

"I'll tell you one thing," Steve said softly as a cab pulled up. "I've never seen you like this before, and I never want to see you like this again!"

After a long day with Emma, who'd woken up early and hadn't napped, Nina decided to give her an early dinner and put her to bed. She'd wait for Steve, and they'd eat in the dining room for a change.

But she kept snacking on Emma's leftovers and then wasn't hungry. Emma was so over-tired that she wouldn't go to sleep. She didn't want a story, and she certainly didn't want Nina to sing to her. Nina decided to show her a cartwheel. When she was six or seven she'd seen someone do cartwheels on television and she'd been determined to learn. She'd practiced every day. It was the first thing she could remember really working hard on. In high school she'd been a cheerleader, and for a few years after that she'd do an occasional cartwheel for herself or, after a few drinks, for a boyfriend. She couldn't remember the last time she'd done one.

In the middle of moving the coffee table she began to regret she'd gotten Emma interested, but it was too late. So despite feeling full, she stretched and tried to limber up. Her skirt felt so tight she took it off and then, to Emma's delight, she took off her sweater, too.

She discovered she still could do a pretty decent cartwheel. And it still made her feel happy and free.

Emma laughed, clapped, made her do another—which wasn't as good—and then went happily to bed.

Nina thought about leaving the furniture and greeting Steve in her bra and panties. She didn't think she'd ever done a cartwheel for him and wasn't sure he even knew she could do them. It was just the kind of thing he'd be charmed by, especially if she did it in her underwear. One night when they'd first known each other and he'd called to say he'd be home early, Nina had put on her black negligee that had many tiny satin-covered buttons down the front. When he'd walked in she didn't say a word but led him to their bedroom. She sat him on their bed and ordered him to close his eyes. Then, spraying perfume in the air as she said, "You can open your eyes now," she walked towards him through the mist and sang "My Funny Valentine."

Afterwards it took him a while, but he undid every one of her tiny buttons.

But now she was tired, and by the time Steve got home she'd put on her clothes and moved back the furniture. She hadn't made the special dinner she'd planned. "I'm not hungry," she told him, "but I'll keep you company."

They sat at the kitchen table, which she'd cleared, but the counters were messy from Emma's dinner and there were piles of dishes in the sink.

"I don't mind mac and cheese, but it's not my favorite," Steve muttered. "Especially when it has tuna-fish and peas in it."

She'd forgotten he didn't like it.

He was wearing a dark grey sweater patterned with large and small blue and turquoise circles. When she'd bought it for him he'd teased that it made him look like a nerd whose wife was trying to liven him up. "You look adorable!" she'd said, but now he just looked tired. They'd been up late the past few nights writing application essays, and although he denied it, she suspected that the seemingly endless process was hard on him, too.

He dropped his napkin and as he bent down to pick it up, she noticed a spot where his hair was beginning to thin. She wondered if he knew it was there. He seemed vulnerable and she felt fiercely protective, the way she did towards Emma.

"How was your day?" she asked him.

"Long."

He had a large practice and usually enjoyed his work. Occasionally when they were out they'd run into an adolescent who was or had been his patient. Although the kids tended to be shy, reticent or startled to see him out of context, she could tell they liked him.

She kept absent-mindedly nibbling bits of dried macaroni from the sides of the serving bowl.

"Do you want me to get you a plate?" Steve asked her.

She knew that if she weren't there he'd watch the World Series.

But she'd barely spoken to another adult all day. She smelled her wrist to see if she'd remembered to put on perfume. She hadn't. Since his outburst after Emma's interview, Nina had been trying to be more cheerful. She could tell him about her cartwheel, but then he'd want to see it … she decided to save it for some dreary day when she'd be older and less desirable.

By the time they'd finished all the applications and interviews, it was late fall. On nice days Nina and Emma would go to a playground in Central Park. Sometimes as they walked there Nina would sing a song about the red, yellow and brown leaves falling down; sometimes Emma would not only let her finish it but join in, her voice small but clear. Near the playground gate the air would be full of children's voices, and Nina would always see an old man in a wheelchair sleeping with his mouth open. The young woman who looked after him would be talking on her phone.

It was a small playground. Emma loved climbing the big stone hippos and Nina found it easy to talk to moms she didn't know. They told funny stories about raising children and gave lots of good advice. They'd often talk about their personal lives. When they'd complain about their husbands Nina would complain too, but only about little things like the way Steve, trying to throw his dirty socks in the hamper, would leave whatever fell on the floor for her to pick up. Occasionally there'd be a scary story, like the child whose fever was so high the thermometer broke. "I assumed it was defective," his mother said, "but when we got a new one, the same thing happened." The story had a happy ending, but then another mother said, "You think that's bad? Wait 'til she doesn't get invited to a birthday party."

Nina liked watching the few dads who'd be there. One, who looked as if he'd played college football not so long before, always held his small son's hand as they walked from one activity to another. There was an adoring gray-haired man with a little girl about a year younger than Emma. One day Nina told him how much she liked his granddaughter's apparently unlimited supply of fancy sweaters.

"Actually," he said, "I'm her dad."

Nina wasn't sure what to say.

He smiled. "Life is good!"

Suddenly ashamed of how obsessed she'd been with what was, after all, only preschool, Nina felt how lucky she was to have Emma and Steve.

"Thank you so much for reminding me!" she told the dad.

And although she could tell he was secretly looking at her breasts—the sun had come out and she'd opened her jacket—it was all she could do not to give him a hug.

In January she got a call to say that Heidi, an acquaintance Nina's age who sang in children's libraries, was in the hospital: could Nina sub for her a few days later?

Nina had vowed not to sing in places like nursing homes or any place that involved children. But she hadn't performed anywhere since before Emma was born, she had nothing else planned that day, and maybe Emma would enjoy it.

When the morning came she tried on a scarlet tee shirt she sometimes wore for exercising. It had a big yellow chicken on the front and Emma loved it, but when Nina saw herself in the mirror she hated looking so sexless and ended up wearing the somewhat loose skirt and top she'd worn to a preschool interview. At the last minute she put on high-heeled boots.

The Children's Room didn't have many books on display, and although there were a few posters of baby animals on the walls, it wasn't particularly cheerful. Nina had never taken Emma to libraries where people lined up for hours for children's events and even, she'd heard, forged tickets; this clearly wasn't one of them. The librarian was grateful she was there.

Soon there was a steady stream of children with their moms and nannies. Everyone sat on the floor in a circle that kept expanding for latecomers. Nina gave Emma juice and raisins and hoped she'd be quiet. A mom Nina recognized from the playground was there with her son. When an attractive dad in a dark brown leather jacket came in—he looked French or Italian—with a pretty little girl, Nina automatically smiled at him.

She began with "Itsy, Bitsy Spider," which she and Emma had sung at various children's shows. Many of the children joined her. She'd worried that Emma would yell at her to Stop! But although Emma looked a little dazed, she quietly sipped her juice. Nina led everyone in "Twinkle, Twinkle, Little Star." A few of the parents joined in, and she could hear the attractive dad's deep voice. The librarian gave out tambourines, maracas, triangles and drums, and during "You Are My Sunshine" the children shook their instruments; a few even kept the beat. Nina realized she was having a good time. At one point she became aware that she was sneaking looks at the dad and made herself stop. After everyone acted out "If You're Happy and You Know It" and "The Wheels on the Bus," Nina glanced at her watch and was surprised that her time was almost up. She ended with a goodbye-and-see-you-soon song, pausing for each child to fill in his or her name. Sometimes the parent or nanny would have to say it, but Emma said her name in such a bold, confident way, Nina had to blink back tears. The attractive dad's daughter was Laura. Nina couldn't place his accent.

Sitting down to a lot of applause, she felt that her cheeks were flushed. She smelled her own perfume.

"Good job!" a boy behind her said loudly. Nina and several adults nearby laughed. The familiar-looking mom came over, and as she was saying how much she'd liked the show, for a second Nina had the wild hope she was somehow connected to the admissions committee of their first-choice school.

As Nina helped Emma put on her jacket, she wondered if Laura and her dad were still there…she wanted him to come over and make her feel pretty and talented and alluring…but when she let herself turn to look, they were gone. She decided that was just as well.

At dinner that night Nina was pleased to have something new to talk to Steve about.

"Were you proud of your beautiful mommy?" he asked Emma.

Licking ketchup from her fingers, she gave him a big smile.

As Nina did the dishes she could hear Emma's shrieks of laughter as Steve played with her. Sometimes when he took over and Nina was free to take a break she'd linger in the doorway, reluctant to tear herself away from the pleasure of seeing them together.

When Emma was in bed Nina mentioned Laura's dad to Steve, and he seemed gratifyingly half-jealous. For the first time in months, they talked about having a second child. She was still conflicted because part of her wanted to use the time Emma would be in school to work on her career. Steve wanted another child, but he was understanding about her ambivalence. He talked about expanding his practice and taking in a partner. They went to bed early.

"Do you still love me?" she asked after they made love.

"I do."

After their difficult autumn, she didn't dare ask coyly, as she'd sometimes ask when they'd make up after a fight, "Do you love me more?"

In March Emma was accepted by their second and third choice schools and wait-listed for their first.

Steve admitted he was relieved. He bought whipped cream, maraschino cherries and chocolate syrup and made Emma her first ice cream sundae. Later he and Nina ate take-out Thai food and had champagne. Although they'd gone over the pros and cons of their first and second choice schools many times, they decided that in some ways they were better off not having gotten what they wanted. For the first time in a long time, they made love two nights in a row. And a few nights later, for the first time in weeks they had a date night.

The only reservation she could get was at 9:30, and by then they were tired and hungry. There were couples close-by on either side of them. A few tables away was a couple with a little boy whose voice was loud and shrill.

Their waiter finally appeared and as he went over the specials he flirted a little with Nina. Steve didn't seem to notice. Although they'd vowed not to talk about Emma's new school, every few minutes one of them would forget. After a while they stopped speaking.

One of the couples beside them was clearly on a first date; the other couple seemed to be enjoying each other's company. Nina wondered if they were all promising themselves they'd never end up like her and Steve.

"I'm glad this school business is over, at least for now," he said. "We've got to do better next time."

She knew that he meant just her and was probably cranky because he was hungry, and that she should change the subject before they had a fight. But she was hungry and cranky too.

"Sorry, but you were acting like such a jerk about it," Steve said. "Letting it get to you like that."

"What did you call me?"

As soon as their waiter brought drinks and their food Steve started eating.

Nina just sat there. "I can't believe you called me a jerk," she said. She was aware the other couples could hear her, but she didn't care.

"That wasn't what I meant. It's just…you know how crazy you were." He was eating quickly.

She didn't even pick up her fork. "I'm not one of your

buddies, you know. I'm not your roommate."

"I shouldn't have said it, you know how I get when I'm hungry."

"It's like you called me an asshole."

"Can we just let it go?"

She shook her head slowly. "I can't believe you called me a jerk."

"God, you're like a pit bull."

"Is that what you see me as, some feral animal?"

"I do not see you as a feral animal."

One couple next to them was getting ready to go. Nina realized that the shrill little boy was gone, too.

Steve's plate was empty. "You're not going to eat anything?" he asked her.

She started eating, slowly. Even though her food was barely warm it was delicious, but she was too angry to enjoy it.

"Nina? Sweetie?"

She wouldn't look at him.

"I'm really sorry," he said.

"Only a man can be a jerk," she muttered. "It's like only a man can be an asshole."

He reached across the table for her hand. She put it in her lap.

"What can a woman be?" he asked her.

She thought about it. "A bitch."

He smiled. "Well, you're not a bitch."

"And I'll tell you something else," she said. "I'm tired of picking up your stupid socks when you try to throw them in the hamper and miss."

He looked puzzled. "Fine," he said finally. "From now on, every night when I take off my socks I'll carefully deposit them in the hamper."

As they waited for coffee Nina thought about the way he'd sit on the bed in his underwear and aim each sock at the hamper: it seemed boyish and…hopeful.

"You know what, forget what I said. I don't mind picking them up."

"What?"

"I really don't mind picking up your socks."

He looked exasperated.

"Promise me you won't stop throwing them in the hamper."

"Can we change the subject?"

"Promise me."

He shrugged.

Barely drinking their coffee, they left.

It had rained while they were eating, and the wet street under the streetlights looked romantic to her. "Let's walk home."

"What about the sitter?"

"Please."

After a while, she reached for his hand.

As they neared their building, she said, "Listen, we have to be careful." She could feel him tense, but couldn't stop herself. "I read somewhere, or maybe I heard it, someone said that there are three kinds of couples with kids…."

He sighed exaggeratedly.

"No, listen, it's important. For some marriages, children don't make any difference in the couple's relationship. And some marriages actually get better when they have kids. But some marriages…"

They were in the middle of the street, but he stopped

walking. "Okay. I get it." He let go of her hand. "And you know what else? I've fucking had it with your fucking horror stories!"

It wasn't even 5:00 on a Sunday morning in April when Emma climbed into their bed, wide-awake and eager to play. It was Nina's turn to get up with her. "Bye!" said Steve, turning away from them.

After breakfast they read many books and played a few games. It was just getting light, but Nina had run out of things for them to do that wouldn't wake Steve. So despite the damp cold, she took Emma out.

On Broadway a Sunday Times had blown all over the sidewalk and into the street. The city already looked tired to Nina as she pushed the stroller slowly and tried to kill time.

She finally found an open coffee shop and bought Emma juice, which she immediately spilled. She had a tantrum and Nina finally took her out. There was a pale sun and she headed to Central Park.

The playground hadn't opened yet, so Nina and Emma—who'd calmed down and was eating old raisins she'd found in her stroller—sat on a nearby bench. Soon many other families were filling the other benches. Nina wondered if one day there'd be a line to get into the playground. Ellen was right about the city getting too crowded. Since it was the weekend there were more dads than usual. Nina tried to tell which ones were divorced and which were letting their wives sleep late. When a mom with a son around Emma's age sat near them, Nina hoped she'd ask where Emma would be going to school: when she told her, the woman would be impressed. Ashamed, she thought about calling Steve to say, "I just realized I'm no better than any other bragging parent!" But she wasn't sure he'd be up. She also worried he'd use it as ammunition during their next fight.

She and Emma enjoyed watching a man with a big ring full of keys unlock the playground gate. When he opened it, Emma ran in.

Nina ran after her, then sat on a bench in the sun. It was still cool, but definitely getting warmer. A familiar-looking dad came in with his familiar-looking daughter. Nina found a few more old raisins in Emma's stroller and ate them. Emma was kicking a plastic ball that didn't seem to belong to anyone. After a while it rolled near the familiar-looking man, and Nina realized he was the dad she'd mistaken for a grandfather. Something was different, though. His hair was black. He must have dyed it! She wished he hadn't.

"Is life still good?" she wanted to ask him.

He picked up Emma's ball and threw it gently to her.

There was a slight breeze that made it veer a little, but Emma reached right out and caught it.

"Good job!" Nina called out. She couldn't wait to tell Steve.

Little Ghost Face

Manhattan

While Miranda was waiting for the light to change, she noticed a familiar-looking man standing next to her. Thin, with dark longish hair, he had a big camera around his neck and wore a dress shirt and expensive-looking jeans. He was probably in his late twenties, ten years younger than she. As they crossed the street she realized he'd been the translator for a Q and A at a film festival she'd gone to a few weeks before. She'd found it both annoying and amusing that although the French director gave long, complicated-sounding answers, the translator had barely taken notes and his translations had been, comparatively, brief.

She thought he was attractive, but she was getting divorced, not interested in dating yet—and definitely not in dating a younger man.

They were walking in the same direction. She'd disliked the movie and was curious about what he thought.

He'd disliked it, too.

"You're a translator?"

"Not really." He yawned. "I was there to take pictures, but the translator got sick and I said I'd do it." He yawned again. "My mom was French."

"You're a photographer?"

"Not really."

It was a sunny morning in early July. Seeing the entrance to the High Line she smiled, told him to enjoy the nice day, and walked quickly away.

He kept up with her. "Um, you have something on your tooth." He touched one of his front teeth.

Embarrassed, she picked at her teeth with her fingernail. "Is it gone?"

"All gone."

She was used to being attractive to men and automatically took out her ponytail and shook her head so her light brown hair framed her face. Lately she'd been wearing tops that didn't reveal much cleavage.

"You're going to the High Line?" he asked.

Reluctantly, she nodded.

"It's gonna be mobbed," he said cheerfully. "I live around here and I only go when it first opens or when the weather's bad."

Lucky you, she felt like saying.

He yawned. "Sorry. I'm *tired* today."

She remembered being his age—actually, she'd been younger—and going on about how tired she was.

"You're not a tourist," he said.

"No. It's my first day of vacation, and I've been meaning to get back here for months." She wished she'd just said, No.

"Have you ever been on the Paris High Line?" he asked her.

"I don't think so." She'd gone to Paris with her ex-husband, but they'd only had time for the main tourist attractions.

"It's called the Promenade Plantée. It's a lot less crowded. You should go."

Although she was a lawyer and could afford to go back, it annoyed her that he was one of those privileged people who assume everyone is like them.

They were at the Highline staircase.

"Take it easy." She walked up quickly.

He was right next to her. "Actually, if I go back to my apartment I'll take a nap and then I'll wake up in a bad mood. The High Line will probably put me in a worse mood, but it'll keep me awake." He smiled. "I'm Matt."

The walkway was crowded as far as she could see.

"Miranda," she said reluctantly.

There were so many people on the walkway, and so many of them kept stopping to take pictures, that Miranda and Matt had to sort of shuffle along.

"I told you it would be bad," he said.

Despite the crowds, she enjoyed the plantings and the city views.

Every few minutes Matt yawned noisily or muttered about having warned her. Miranda wondered if he had a girlfriend. If he did, she felt sorry for her.

Several blocks later, just as they were approaching the wooden lounge chairs, a couple who'd been sitting there stood up. Miranda was afraid that if she sat down Matt would join her, but the crowds were starting to get to her.

Matt sat down too.

They watched the passersby and tried to figure out which ones were tourists. They agreed that no one—no matter how attractive or well dressed—looks good wearing a backpack. Several pretty women walked by.

"We should give these chairs to someone else," Miranda said after a while.

"But everyone's *sightseeing*—they're *walking*—it's not like we're in a *restaurant* and people are waiting to eat."

Once when she and her ex-husband, also a lawyer, were approaching the dining room of a trendy restaurant, he speeded up (he later denied this) so he could claim the only available table before a woman with a cane could get there.

"So, Miranda, what do you do besides go to film festivals and the High Line?"

He was what her dad would call a pip. "I'm a real estate lawyer."

She wondered how he'd react if she added that she was planning to have a child by artificial insemination. He'd probably assume she wanted him to be a sperm donor. *Don't flatter yourself*, she'd say.

"So you're not a translator…or a photographer?"

Suddenly animated, Matt said he was fascinated by the technical aspects of photography, but worried that his pictures were clichéd. His father owned a factory that made toiletries for prisons and hospitals. "I sort of enjoy doing spreadsheets, but I'm afraid that if I end up working for my father, I'll hate myself."

He sounded like he'd had a lot of therapy.

She stood up.

As soon as Matt stood, too, two older women rushed to take their seats.

Matt and Miranda shuffled along until they came to the next staircase

"I've had it with these crowds!" she said abruptly. "Enjoy the rest of your day."

He followed her down the stairs. "You look kind of white," he said when they were on the street. "Are you okay?"

"Maybe it's my sunscreen." She'd gotten ready quickly and hoped she hadn't been careless. She was also anxious about having a child on her own and hadn't been sleeping well. She took out her mirror.

"You're right," she said. "I look like a ghost." Suddenly—as had been happening lately—she was close to tears. "Do you enjoy making people feel bad about things they can't help?" She hadn't meant to say it.

They were almost at her subway station.

"Gotta go," she said. "Maybe we'll run into each other on the High Line some day when the weather's really bad."

"Wait! I'm sorry. I think you're really pretty."

"Forget it."

"My shrink once told me it's not enough to just apologize—you have to do something to make it up to the person. Let me buy you lunch."

"That's nice of you, but I need to get home."

"Don't go." He smiled. He had a boyish smile. "Please."

She suspected he just didn't like to be alone. It wasn't her problem.

"Let me buy you lunch and then you'll never have to see me again."

There was something touching about his putting it that way, as if he understood how annoying he could be. She was also hungry.

"I'll buy my own lunch," she said finally.

They ended up at a crowded, over-priced restaurant where it took a long time to get their food. After a while, they began to talk more personally.

It turned out that his mother had died when he was

eleven. Miranda's had died when she was twelve.

When he told her his ex-girlfriend had gone back to an old boyfriend, he seemed so sad that Miranda liked him better.

"When I was unhappy my dad used to say, 'It's only a life,'" she said.

"I bet you'd be unhappy about things like getting A- instead of A. I bet you went to an Ivy League college."

She smiled. She suspected he'd gone to some expensive liberal arts college that wasn't well-enough known to be useful in the job market.

"And I bet you're close to your dad."

He wasn't stupid.

When their food finally came, she kept surreptitiously checking her teeth.

She let him pay.

"I have a crazy idea," he said when they got outside. He wanted her to cash in her flyer miles—"I bet you've got plenty"—and use her vacation days to go with him to his family's pied-à-terre in Paris. "There's a sofa bed and a cot. I'll show you the Promenade Plantée."

"That's really sweet of you, but it's out of the question."

"You're on vacation. Listen, two days for travel, five days there—it would just be a week." He smiled. "And then you'll never have to see me again."

"I have plans. But thank you. And thanks again for lunch."

"Will you think about it? Promise you'll at least think about it."

She let him give her his email.

All night she kept waking up, anxious about choosing

a sperm donor, worried that like many women her age, she'd need fertility treatments. On the other hand, if it turned out that she was okay, she could have a child fairly soon, and then it might be years before she'd have another real vacation. Matt could be annoying, and her friends would say she was crazy, but she'd made few vacation plans and had plenty of miles, and she could always move to a hotel. And if things worked out, she'd not only get to know Paris better, but her trip would basically be free.

Paris

Although Miranda was disappointed when her taxi pulled up in front of an ordinary-looking building in the 12th arrondissement, she was relieved when Matt, who'd arrived a few hours earlier, came down to let her in. His hair was damp as if he'd just showered, and his expensive-looking tee shirt and linen shorts looked fresh. As she stood close to him in the tiny elevator, she suddenly worried that as her friends had predicted, there was only one bed.

But although the studio was small, there was a sofa and also a tiny alcove with just enough room for the cot. In the small kitchen area there was nothing on the shelves but a cookie tin and a photo of a little boy who looked like Matt, wearing glasses and standing between a husky man and a slender blonde woman Miranda assumed was Matt's mom. She looked younger than Miranda.

"Is that your mom?" she asked Matt. "She's very pretty."

He just nodded.

Miranda managed to shower—there wasn't much

water pressure—and changed into a new dress (with a neckline that wasn't too revealing). Wiping the condensation from the small window, she saw the sun behind the clouds.

"I know I said I'd take you to the Promenade," Matt said when she came out, "but I'm really tired. Do you mind if I take a nap first?"

She hadn't slept much on the plane and realized she was tired, too.

He opened the sofa bed and showed her how to deal with the tricky latch. She pretended to listen, but could hardly keep her eyes open. The next thing she knew it was early afternoon, cloudy, and Matt was crawling on the floor muttering, Shit!

"I dropped my stupid contact lens."

She got down on the dusty floor and looked with him, but she couldn't find it either.

She remembered how when she was a counselor, one camper or another was always losing a contact lens.

"Shit! Shit! Shit!"

"Do you have glasses?"

"Yes I have glasses."

She hesitated. "Did you bring them?"

"Yes I brought them." He stood up. "I hate wearing glasses. I only wear sunglasses."

He sounded like a spoiled child. She doubted he'd ever had a summer job. She wondered how much of the next three days she was obligated to spend with him.

As soon as they went out she saw a young man carrying a baguette with the end bitten off. And right on Matt's block was an ancient-looking store that repaired musical instruments, a boulangerie (closed for vacation), and a boutique with several attractive leather jackets in the window. It was humid, but it looked as if the sun might come out again.

Matt, wearing sunglasses that apparently weren't prescription, found a café that didn't seem touristy. He ordered ham sandwiches for both of them, and then he and the waitress had a long discussion in French.

"She doesn't like the way the neighborhood is gentrifying," he told Miranda when the waitress had gone.

"Your French sounds so natural."

"Not to anyone who's French," he said glumly.

She wanted to look in his eyes and say something comforting, but he'd kept on his sunglasses.

She'd never eaten ham with sweet butter, and she loved it. She imagined making it for her child. It felt odd to be in Paris, thinking about her child. She tried not to eat too quickly, but Matt was really slow. Looking at herself in the mirror on her phone, she surreptitiously checked her teeth.

The waitress gave Matt the bill. He told Miranda they should split it.

"I'll treat you to something fancier tonight," she said.

"You'd better."

He left more than half of his baguette. When he walked out ahead of her she had an impulse to break off a piece and quickly stuff it in her mouth, but she wasn't hungry.

They didn't have far to walk before they came to the stairs for the Promenade.

There were empty benches, plantings, and plenty of room for the few people—who looked like locals—walking and jogging.

"I love it," she said right away.

"You have to agree, this makes you hate the High Line."

She took a lot of pictures. Matt had his big camera around his neck, but didn't even take the cap off.

"Do you know something else I hate?" he asked her. "I hate the way some women sign their emails to everyone XO."

They'd emailed a few times about the trip; Miranda hoped she hadn't automatically signed hers that way.

"And another thing—how do you know which is hugs and which is kisses?"

She couldn't tell if in some weird way he was flirting. "I think the X is kisses and the O is hugs."

"But then it would be kisses and hugs instead of hugs and kisses."

Miranda pulled her hair into a ponytail.

The sun came out. She kept going to the sides of the walkway to take pictures of the streets below, which seemed more a part of the neighborhood than the gentrified ones around the High Line. She wished she could tell her ex about the Promenade, but she'd been the one to end the marriage—partly when she realized she didn't want to raise a child with him—and he hated her now.

"You know the fable about the sun and the wind?" Matt asked her.

She was taking pictures and didn't answer. In the middle of the street below a cyclist and a taxi driver were gesticulating and yelling, but their voices were faint and she wouldn't have understood them anyway.

"So the sun and the wind are having this argument about who's more powerful. Then they see a man walking down the road and they decide to have a contest to see who can get him to take off his coat."

Miranda kept taking pictures. She wished he would, too.

"So the wind blows harder and harder, and the man just buttons up his coat. Then the sun beats down on him. And guess what?"

"I don't know." If he was trying to obliquely communicate something about himself, or her, or about him and her, she didn't get it.

"Can you guess?"

"The man takes off his coat."

"Exactly!" He looked happy. "Is that the stupidest fable you ever heard?"

"I guess."

By the time they got back to where they'd started it was getting dark, but Matt kept on his sunglasses.

He couldn't find the bistro he remembered from his childhood, and they had to settle for a restaurant that was crowded with tourists.

As they looked at the French-English menu, an old man began to play Piaf songs on the guitar, and another old man tried to sell Matt a rose. A young woman who looked like a gypsy and carried a sleeping baby circled the room, holding out her hand.

"Paris in July," Matt muttered. Then he pretty much stopped talking—except to say, when Miranda ordered rabbit, "In July?"

He ordered some kind of fish, which their French waiter seemed to approve of.

Miranda tried to figure out which, if any, of the other customers were Parisians, but Matt wasn't interested in guessing.

"I suppose you know that the Promenade Plantée was the first High Line," she said.

Matt looked gloomy.

"Is something wrong?"

He shook his head.

She hoped that the German families sitting on either side of them didn't think she was paying him for sex.

"I can't remember where I read it," she said, "but someone said that the French are like the Italians, only in a bad mood." She smiled.

He didn't respond.

"Do you feel okay?" He looked a little pale.

"I feel fine."

Then take off your stupid sunglasses.

Miranda tried to pace herself when her food came, but Matt just picked at his fish. Finishing her second glass of wine—Matt had barely touched his first—she counted the number of meals they had left.

"I guess I'm not that hungry," Matt said. He pushed his plate away.

The waiter gave him the bill. He passed it to Miranda. Taking out her credit card, she felt self-conscious.

As they walked back to Matt's apartment and she again admired the leather jackets in the boutique window, she was amazed she hadn't even been in Paris for twenty-four hours.

"I feel sort of funny," Matt said as they went into his building. He ran up the stairs.

Getting out of the elevator, Miranda could hear him vomiting.

"Can I do anything?" she called in the direction of the

bathroom.

"No."

In a way she was relieved there was an excuse for his behavior. After quickly putting on pajamas, she couldn't remember what he'd told her about opening the sofa. She was lying on top of it when he staggered out of the bathroom, pale and sweaty.

"I can go out and get you a Coke or something."

He just groaned. "I hope you don't get whatever this is."

She hoped it wasn't food poisoning from the ham sandwich.

He insisted on opening the sofa for her. Then he practically ran over to the cot, threw himself down, and fell asleep.

She'd meant to ask if there was a fan. She was wondering if she'd be able to fall asleep without one, when she fell asleep.

All night she kept waking up. Matt would be either vomiting in the bathroom or sprawled on the cot, occasionally snoring. She put off using the bathroom, but when she finally went in it looked clean. At dawn, she was wide-awake. She googled nearby hotels. She couldn't tell if she was coming down with whatever he had or was just imagining she was. After a while she got up and looked in the kitchen for something that he might be able to keep down, but the fridge was unplugged and there were just some broken Christmas cookies in the tin. She dressed in the bathroom, in the one dress she'd taken that revealed a little cleavage—she doubted Matt would notice. She was trying and failing to close the sofa bed when he sat up.

"I'll close it," he said, but he didn't move.

She went out and bought Coke and crackers. Although there was a small hotel nearby, she decided that if he still wanted her to, she owed it to him to stay.

He groaned at the crackers, but sipped a little Coke.

"Go out and enjoy Paris," he said.

"I should be here in case you need me."

"I'll probably sleep all day. By the time you come back I'll be hungry and we can get dinner. Your treat, right?"

She wasn't sure what to do. The sofa bed was still open, his clothes were all over the floor, and the air in the room was stale.

"You're sure?"

"Go!"

She couldn't wait to get out of there.

There was a long line outside the Musée D'Orsay, so she spent the drizzly morning walking around and drinking café au lait. She window-shopped and bought a tortoise shell comb that looked like a fish. When the sun came out she put on sunscreen, rubbed it in carefully and walked some more, enjoying the ordinary neighborhoods she and her ex had missed. She decided against another ham sandwich and ate a salade Nicoise for lunch. Remembering Matt's poor little ghost face across the table, she hoped he was feeling better. She ended up on a bench in a small park. An old man was selling balloons, and she watched the children playing with them. Before she knew it, she might have her own child. "Look what Mommy got in Paris!" she'd say, holding up her comb that looked like a fish. A bride and groom posed in front of a small garden of daisies. A group of Japanese tourists lined up at the water fountain. She meant to just close her eyes, but she fell asleep. When she woke up it was late afternoon and for a few terrifying seconds, she had no idea where she was.

Matt had given her keys, but she knocked. When he opened the door he was holding a map and wearing black rectangular glasses.

"All better!" he said. He'd closed the sofa, picked up his clothes, and put in a window fan. "Remember that restaurant I was looking for?" He showed her where it was on the map. "I'm starving."

His hair was damp from a shower. He wore a linen shirt with the sleeves rolled up and tight jeans. No longer so pale, he seemed, as her dad would say, bright eyed and bushy tailed.

"You look good in glasses!" Miranda told him.

"You look pretty good yourself." He was staring at her cleavage.

It had been months since she'd had sex. Loosening her hair, she let Matt take her in his arms and press his penis against her.

He showed her his condom, took her hand, and led her to the sofa. When he tried to open it, though, the metal bar got stuck.

"Shit! Shit! Shit!"

It didn't take him long to fix it, but by the time they'd undressed she was no longer in the mood. She couldn't decide whether to tell him to stop. She decided she owed it to him to fake it.

He was a more considerate lover than she would have thought, but she lay under him counting his thrusts, hoping it wouldn't be much longer, and mimicking the way she breathed and the noises she made when she was really excited. Suddenly everything in her life (except her divorce and her job) seemed like a mistake. She wasn't even sure about having the baby. She felt sad and alone. But as Matt came and she pretended she was coming, too, she promised herself that, at the very least, the next time she had sex—she'd mean it.

CANDY APPLE RED

He was a stay-at-home dad and she was a single mom, and they lived in the same New York City suburb. Their two-year old daughters had been in the same music class, but Jake and Ellen didn't talk until their girls were invited to a classmate's birthday party. As soon as he got there Jake was aware of her, across the backyard, because she was the only mom wearing a skirt and high heels. She made him think of a blonde Swiss exchange student who'd come on a high school ski trip, and an Asian woman with long black hair he'd once seen crying on the Long Island Railroad: beside their beauty, what they had in common was that they were out of his league. Beth, his wife, told him he was handsome, but he had a bald spot and wore glasses and thought he looked like someone who'd spent his teenage years obsessed with video games. The late fall Sunday had started out sunny but was becoming cooler; he hoped that Ellen, in her short skirt, wasn't cold.

Birthday girl Nora's mom was sick so her dad, Scott, was leading the children in various games. When a clown appeared and started making balloon animals, Jake found himself next to Ellen. Her auburn hair, which came almost to her shoulders, was damp as if she'd just washed it, and her perfume had an underlying tobacco-y smell he couldn't get enough of.

She pointed out her daughter, Zinnia; he pointed

out Rachel. Ellen gave him a big smile. They moved to a quieter part of the yard.

"I'm trying to remember if you're a single or a stay-at-home dad."

"Stay-at-home." He explained that Beth worked for a consortium of non-profit arts organizations, and he taught urban history. "But I've been on leave to write a book about John Lindsay."

"Lindsay was a mayor, right?"

Beth liked to say he "talked to the one as if lecturing many," so he tried to keep his explanation of Lindsay's importance brief.

Ellen was an event planner. "Lately there've been a lot of bat and bar mitzvahs." She pronounced it "meetzvah."

He stopped himself from going on about how rabbis should be speaking out against the obscene amounts of money parents spend on thirteen-year-olds. He'd never been so aware of a woman's perfume. Beth wore perfume, but only when they went out, and it wasn't like this. His mom's perfume bottles were clustered on her dresser: they looked dusty, and the perfume seemed evaporated or evaporating or dark like unhealthy urine.

Ellen put on lipstick without looking in a mirror. He couldn't remember seeing a woman do that.

"Is it hard on your wife, your spending time with all the moms?"

People always asked him that. Sometimes he thought they were more interested in that than in his book. "We joke about it, but mainly she worries about not being with Rachel."

Ellen's phone rang. "I have to get this—it's my lawyer." She held up her hand for Jake to wait, and didn't talk long. "He's impossible," she said as she got off, presumably referring to her ex-husband. She smiled at Jake. "I know a divorced dad, but you're my first stay-at-home."

He wondered if she'd slept with the dad.

They talked about how lonely being home with a child could be. He told her he'd made up an acronym for stay-at-home-dad. "SAD."

She didn't respond.

He felt too shy to suggest they get the girls together for a playdate.

Zinnia joined them. She had dark curls, but looked like Ellen. "Mommy, I'm hungry."

"You'll have to wait a minute, darling, Mommy's talking."

Jake liked it that Ellen wasn't falling all over herself—like so many moms—to do whatever her child wanted.

"I'm hungry," Zinnia whined.

"There'll be birthday cake soon. Why don't you see what the clown is doing with that big drum."

Zinnia stood there awhile, then did as she was told.

Jake and Ellen talked about a "fourth trimester" group they'd taken their infant girls to (on different days). Ellen had stopped going to hers. "It was like high school, with these cliques of cool moms, prom queen moms, moms who wear overalls…."

Jake suspected she got along better with men. He remembered a description he'd read about some French femme fatale: "She looked like men loved to spoil her."

Ellen touched his arm. "We'd better mingle." She lowered her voice. "Being divorced in such a tiny community, the wives always think you're after their husband."

Jake didn't know what to say.

As she walked away, he liked what her high heels made her do with her hips.

One of the moms from his fourth trimester group came over and introduced him to her husband.

They talked about the Yankees. Jake always felt a little awkward with the husbands and was relieved when Scott called everyone over to sing Happy Birthday.

Jake helped Rachel get her ice cream and cake, and when she sat at the picnic table with the other children he stood behind her with his own plate. Several parents around him were chatting, but he was happy to watch Rachel, who was carefully eating a spoonful of ice cream, then a spoonful of cake. He wasn't sure who she resembled. She had a thin face and big eyes and could look solemn; he thought she was beautiful. Staying home with her was the hardest thing he'd ever done, but also the most gratifying. Sometimes he didn't tell Beth the best moments of the day because he didn't want her to feel left out. When Rachel got up to play with some children she knew, Jake ate her leftovers, despite his resolution to cut down on sweets—since his leave, he'd put on a few pounds.

He and Rachel and Ellen and Zinnia and a few other parents and children were in the kitchen helping clean up, when he heard a mom saying that Maggie, Nora's mom, was gravely ill. As the news spread, a few parents picked up their children and held them close. Jake thought about Rachel losing Beth and felt almost dizzy. He wasn't sure what Maggie looked like. He barely knew Scott, but felt he should say something sympathetic. He wished Beth were with him—she was better at these things—but she was en route to a conference in Miami. Scott was outside, giving out party bags. Jake took advantage of the crush of people to just mouth Thanks and wave goodbye.

He and Rachel were a few blocks away when Ellen, pushing Zinnia in her stroller, rushed up to him.

"I'm so upset," she said, bursting into tears.

Barely touching her shoulder, Jake wanted tc put his arms around her—to offer comfort, but also to sniff her smoky perfume.

"Maggie and I weren't exactly friends, but Zinnia and Nora had a few playdates and we were definitely friendly. I can't believe she never told me she was sick! I mean, I heard she was having health issues, but nothing like this."

He wanted to ask if Maggie had dark hair she wore in a ponytail, but he didn't want to admit he wasn't sure what she looked like. He was finding it hard to concentrate.

"She clearly didn't tell a lot of people," he murmured.

Rachel, strapped in her stroller, was squirming.

"Well, I'm really upset."

Ellen rummaged around in Zinnia's stroller—he noticed she wasn't strapped in—found something that looked like a used napkin, and blew her nose. "Is my eye make-up all runny?"

"You're fine," he said. "Listen, Monday's supposed to be a nice day. I was thinking about taking Rachel to Brighton Beach. Would you and Zinnia like to come?" This wasn't the kind of thing he usually did, especially with someone he didn't know.

"I've never been there," Ellen said.

He enjoyed showing people around New York—Beth teased he should have been a tour guide. He'd particularly enjoy showing Ellen.

"I have to warn you," he said reluctantly, "there can be

traffic…."

"No, we definitely want to go." She ran her fingers through Zinnia's curls. "Don't we, pumpkin?"

Zinnia rubbed her nose.

When Beth called that night and Jake told her about Maggie, she couldn't remember her, either. "I know who Scott is. And I remember Nora. Maggie must have missed a lot of kiddie events, poor thing." She wasn't sure who Ellen was.

He could hear voices in the background. "I sort of invited them to go to Brighton Beach with us Monday."

"Scott and Nora?"

He realized that was what he should have done. "Ellen and Zinnia." He explained how upset Ellen had been. "I guess I wanted to cheer her up."

"Hmm," said Beth.

"What?"

"Basically, Maggie's dying, and Ellen's feelings are hurt because Maggie didn't tell her?"

"That's not fair. Everyone was upset."

"Maybe there's a reason why Maggie didn't confide in her."

Sometimes he thought Beth went overboard with her analyses of people, but he could see her point. "Do you think I should make up some excuse and not take them?" He didn't like to lie and decided that if he cancelled, he and Rachel wouldn't go either.

"Let me think about it."

They talked about her conference. He told her how "well organized" Rachel had been at the party as she ate her spoonful of ice cream and then her spoonful of cake. He knew Beth was smiling.

"Did you send me a picture?"

"I forgot to take one." Beth wouldn't have forgotten.

There was a lot of background noise and she raised her voice. "Gotta go."

"Wait! What should I do about Brighton Beach?"

"Brighton Beach. I'm not sure. I'm not back until Tuesday, and you'll have had a lot of child care by then. Maybe it would be nice for Rachel to have a playdate with what's her name? Zinnia? Maybe you should go. Go."

The houses on Ellen's block were bigger and more expensive than the ones on his, but there were no sidewalks and not enough trees by the curb—two of his pet peeves about the suburbs. Although he'd had a feeling Ellen would keep him waiting, she and Zinnia were standing outside when he arrived. Ellen wore a short skirt, a black leather jacket, and high heels.

They'd barely started, and Jake had just put on a CD of children's songs, when Ellen's phone rang. It seemed to be her ex-husband. As she made child care arrangements, she sounded impatient. "He's impossible," she said when she got off.

Jake worried she'd go on and on about her ex-husband, but she asked about his book. As he described the snow-storm during Lindsay's first term—"Queens famously didn't get plowed for a week"—Zinnia started whining, "I'm hungry." He hoped she wouldn't be a bad influence on Rachel who, so far, wasn't a whiner. Ellen gave both girls slices of apple, and for the rest of the trip whenever one of them got restless she'd give them snacks to keep them more or less quiet. When she asked if he'd had news of Maggie (he hadn't), he worried she'd talk about Maggie and upset him when he was driving, but she just sighed.

"So did the moms discuss things like breast pumps and sore nipples with you?"

"Actually, they did." He felt confused because talking this way with her—the air was full of her perfume—made him uncomfortable in a way he hadn't been with the other moms. His friend Josh, married and with older kids, was always asking smarmy questions about the moms. "They're like colleagues," Jake would say, but Josh never believed him. Beth thought Josh had affairs; Jake wasn't sure.

Ellen was easier to talk to than many of Beth's friends, who had a kind of condescending attitude toward men. The husband of one of Beth's friends liked to say mock-seriously about his wife, "Jen sees it as her duty in life to try to protect the world—from me." Once when Beth and her women friends were talking about how men's anger led to rape and war, Jake had surprised them—and himself—by blurting out, "Women are angry too." He'd paused. "At men!" He got a laugh.

Suddenly there was traffic, but it cleared up quickly. He found parking right near the Coney Island boardwalk. When Ellen saw the water, she touched his arm. "Oh, Jakey!"

His cousin used to call him Jakey when she teased him. Now he was taken aback, but he liked it, too.

They went to Nathan's. Without asking, Ellen took one of his fries. He tried to control himself so he wouldn't wolf them all down. Rachel dropped her hotdog and he had to wait on a long line to get her another. The girls smeared themselves with ketchup and had a great time. After Jake and Ellen cleaned them up and changed their diapers, Jake pushed the strollers and Ellen ran with the girls to the boardwalk.

There weren't a lot of people, so they let the girls run around. Ellen was less anxious about safety than Beth. Jake felt disloyal, but he preferred Ellen's approach. The girls tired themselves out and, back in their strollers, fell asleep. As Jake and Ellen walked toward Brighton Beach, he was aware of men looking at her. He felt both protective toward her and pleased with himself for being beside her.

One of the Russian restaurants on the boardwalk was open and they had coffee. Jake couldn't believe how well everything was working out. Ellen hadn't heard about all the plans to develop Coney Island with luxury high-rises and was gratifyingly upset when he told her. As he talked she took out sunscreen and, without taking her eyes off him, slowly rubbed it on her face and neck. Although he suspected she automatically flirted with every man she was around, he enjoyed watching her.

They'd almost finished their coffee when Rachel and Zinnia woke up. Ellen left the strollers with Jake, who was paying their check, and took the girls to the beach.

By the time he joined them, their shoes were off and they were playing "Ring Around the Rosie." With "all fall down," they sank in the sand. Ellen's skirt billowed around her. Jake thought she looked like a princess in a fairy tale.

"Take off your shoes!" she called to him. "Join us."

"I'd rather watch."

Each time they'd all fall down, Jake would clap. "More!" the girls would yell. Ellen would take their hands, and around they'd go again. Beth had definitely judged Ellen too harshly.

Almost as soon as they started back there was heavy

traffic. The girls were cranky. Jake put on a CD for them, but it didn't help. When Ellen twisted around to read to them, they only quieted down for a few minutes; it was as if they were egging each other on. He became aware that one of them had a smelly diaper. It overpowered Ellen's perfume.

"I'll call and we'll make a playdate," Ellen said when he pulled up to her house.

He was sure she wouldn't, and that—just like when he was dating—he'd be too shy to call her.

A few days later it was much colder, and a few days after that, Maggie died. Her picture was in the local paper. Her dark hair was in a ponytail, and she was smiling. She looked familiar and Jake definitely saw how Nora resembled her, but he didn't think they'd ever talked. It felt like a time of endings. Rachel was speaking in longer sentences and was interested in using the potty. In less than a year she'd be in preschool, he'd be back at work, and a part of his life would be over. If they had another child, he wouldn't stay home again.

Perhaps because Beth had been away and then was busy at work, they hadn't really talked since she'd come home. They kept planning date nights, but then something would come up and they'd have to postpone. When they finally did get a sitter, she could only come late so he and Beth just went out for coffee.

The only place open was Starbucks. As Jake complained about all the new chain stores in town, he could tell that Beth wasn't really listening. He realized he complained about this every time they went someplace like Starbucks. It was time for him to go back to work.

Beth yawned. "Sorry, it's been a long day." She ran her fingers through her short dark curls. She'd once told Jake that short curly hair was the best kind for a woman to have when she got gray. He decided she was just as pretty as Ellen, but there was something about her feet that made it hard for her to wear heels, and although she'd occasionally wear skirts to work, she preferred pants—and then as soon as she got home, she'd change into sweats.

Beth talked about a colleague. "Now that she got her promotion, she's really worried about finding a husband." She touched Jake's hand. "We're so lucky."

It always surprised him that she considered him (and of course Rachel) her luck; he didn't know why, but he didn't find it flattering.

"I signed us up to bring meals to Scott and Nora," she told him.

He'd meant to do that.

"You never said much about Brighton Beach."

He described the car-ride-from-hell home.

He was about to drink his coffee when Beth asked if it was decaf—he'd been having trouble sleeping and had decided not to have caffeine at night.

He looked at his cup. "I forgot." He took a sip. "Next time."

"You seem a little edgy."

"I'm fine."

"This awful business with Maggie has upset everyone."

"I'm fine. I never even knew her."

"You're in a good mood," she said.

Sometimes after he'd been alone with Rachel all day, he wouldn't even know he was in a bad mood until Beth got home.

"I really wouldn't mind getting you a decaf," she said. "There's hardly a line."

"I ordered this." He took a few sips. "And I'll tell you something else." He drank it all. "I am not going to be one of those egg-white-omelet-and-decaf-latte-with-skim-milk men walking around with a yoga mat. Not yet, at least." He was surprised by his vehemence.

"Fine," she said. "Can you keep your voice down?"

She looked tired and he felt bad. "Sorry if I've been a grouch."

Beth nodded, but he could tell by way she held her mouth that they wouldn't be having sex.

Lying awake that night, he remembered the morning she'd called him at school to tell him she was pregnant. They hadn't been married long and weren't seriously try-ing, but he was thrilled. Her pregnancy had been a happy time for them. Sometimes out of the blue she'd whisper in his ear, "You knocked me up!" They'd both found that exciting. Now the only thing he regretted about having Rachel was that Beth no longer said it.

A few weeks later Rachel was at her sitter's and Jake was working in his study when Ellen called. It was the first time he'd heard from her since Brighton Beach.

"Sweetie, it's not an emergency, but I need a favor. Are you busy?"

He looked at his computer. "No."

"Can you possibly come over?"

"Of course."

"I'll explain when you get here."

"I'm on my way." He realized he hadn't said that Rachel was at her babysitter's and he almost called her back, but it all seemed too complicated.

As he got out of the car Ellen ran out of the house, putting on a red coat. Her hair was damp as if she'd just washed it. She looked very pretty.

"Where's Rachel?"

"At the sitter."

"Shit! I just assumed the girls could play."

"Where's Zinnia?"

"Napping. Listen, I'm doing this huge bar mitzvah and the caterer switched times on me. I called everyone, but I couldn't get a sitter. I thought you'd bring Rachel."

He was confused, and then he couldn't believe she wanted him to babysit, and then he was furious.

"I left fruit in the kitchen. I'll only be gone an hour, at most an hour and a half."

She ran to her car before he could say that she'd better not be any later.

Beth had been right about her. And her "impossible" husband could doubtless give him an earful. As he walked toward the open front door he imagined it slamming shut and locking before he got in. Zinnia would start scream- ing, and he'd have to call 911. But the door stayed open, and when he got inside all was quiet.

The living room had blond wood furniture, and there were a lot of small and large shocking pink pillows. He preferred a more old-fashioned look, but he'd never had to think about decorating because his in-laws had a large antique-filled house, and they'd been generous to him and Beth. He saw that Ellen hadn't bothered to clean up; sev- eral toys and three small sneakers were scattered around the floor. He sat in a not particularly comfortable chair.

Although there were magazines on the coffee table, and a few bookshelves with not a lot of books, he wished he'd brought his computer. He couldn't believe he wasn't in his study working.

He was about to call Rachel's sitter to warn her he might be late, when he heard Zinnia. Realizing he didn't even know where her room was, he ran upstairs. Right away he saw a closed door decorated with a wooden bouquet of brightly colored flowers he assumed were zinnias. Zinnia was talking quietly to herself and occasionally singing. There were several open doors. The first one he looked into smelled of Ellen's perfume. He started to walk in, but as soon as he saw the big unmade bed he walked out, heart pounding. He told himself to go back and see if he could find the name of her perfume. But he knew that what he'd do was paw through her underwear. Zinnia was crying.

He knocked gently at her door. "It's Rachel's dad. Your mom will be back soon. Can I come in?"

There was what he imagined was a shocked silence, and then she started sobbing. He doubted Ellen had bothered to prepare her for his being there.

"I'm going to open the door now."

As soon as Zinnia saw him she started wailing for her mother. He felt sorry for her.

There were toys and books all over the floor; he saw a puzzle that Rachel had. Zinnia wouldn't let him pick her up, but she finally agreed to have a snack. "Go fish," she kept saying, until he figured out she meant goldfish crackers. He was proud of himself.

"Rachel likes goldfish too."

Zinnia held out her arms for him to pick her up. She

felt lighter than Rachel, and although she'd stopped crying, she still shuddered from her sobs. When she put her head on his shoulder and let him pat her back, he felt a kind of love for her.

She insisted on walking downstairs. She did it more skillfully than Rachel, who tended to be a little fearful. He was surprised by how competitive he felt.

The kitchen was neat. There were apples and a knife on the counter. He gave Zinnia a few slices and they looked for the crackers. When he couldn't find them he started kidding around, pretending to look in places like inside the stove and the garbage can. As she laughed uproariously, he'd alternate between feeling guilty that Rachel wasn't there and being flattered that Zinnia found him so funny. He felt the way he did with Rachel: he loved to make her laugh.

He couldn't find the crackers, but there was a container of ice cream in the back of the freezer. He gave himself and Zinnia big scoops. They ate at the kitchen table, in a kind of companionable silence. It was odd being with a little girl who wasn't Rachel—almost like a date. When Ellen arrived, flushed and slightly out of breath, Zinnia burst into tears.

"We were really fine," he said defensively.

"I got almost everything done. I'm so grateful to you." Still in her coat, she picked up Zinnia. "I'm going to make this up to you," she told Jake. "You'll see." She kept kissing Zinnia. "Can I at least make you coffee?"

"I don't want to be late getting Rachel," he said primly. He had plenty of time.

"I'm going to call you in a few days and have Rachel over, and then you can go out and I'll babysit."

He thought that with anyone else he would have said

forget it, but he wanted Ellen to pay him back. Actually, although she'd only been gone an hour, he'd make it a point to stay out even longer. The idea of taking advantage of her pleased him.

A few days later Ellen called to ask if he and Rachel were free that afternoon, and they were.

She was on the phone as she answered the door. He was disappointed she was wearing pants, but at least they were close-fitting. Her blouse was bright green and she wore many bracelets. Zinnia was drawing at the dining room table. Jake felt close to her, as if they'd had a little adventure together. Ellen, still on the phone, gave Rachel some paper and markers. Jake decided that if Rachel didn't want him to go he'd reluctantly stay. But surprisingly, she didn't mind his leaving.

When he got home he felt too unsettled to work, and he wasn't in the mood to do laundry. He got an email from his college roommate: his pregnant wife and her mother had been walking in Central Park when his mother-in-law was hit by a speeding cyclist. She wasn't expected to live. Jake had met her only once, but he'd liked her. Life seemed precarious and full of sorrow. Not wanting to be alone, he went back to Ellen's.

She looked happy to see him and didn't ask why he was early. As she led him to the kitchen, there was an increasingly strong, somewhat medicinal smell he didn't recognize. Rachel and Zinnia were at the table, which was full of goldfish crackers and bottles of pink, red and purple nail polish. Rachel showed him her red fingernails and toenails. "I have candy! I have candy!"

"Candy Apple Red," Ellen explained. "It's the name of

the polish."

Zinnia, more blasé, had deep purple fingernails and light purple toenails.

Ellen was barefoot. Her nails were red and sparkly. Beth painted her toenails, but only in the summer, and they weren't sparkly.

"We've been very busy," Ellen told him. "We washed and dried each other's feet, and then the girlies got pedicures." She turned toward Rachel and Zinnia. 'I've got an idea," she mock-whispered. "Should we paint Rachel's daddy's toes, too?"

He didn't like people touching his feet. "Sorry, I know lots of men get pedicures, but I'm definitely not into them."

Ellen shrugged, but Rachel kept begging him and she looked so disappointed when he said No that he finally said, "OK, but just one toenail." He'd taken a shower that morning and was fairly sure his toenails weren't disgusting.

Ellen put a basin of soapy water at his feet, then turned on the radio to a station that played lite jazz.

The warm water was soothing, and the messy kitchen seemed cozy. He liked being there, with all the colorful bottles of polish and the clink of Ellen's bracelets. He even liked the medicinal smell mingling with her perfume.

Rachel and Zinnia had fun washing his feet. Although their small fingers made him ticklish, he didn't mind. Ellen's phone kept ringing, and she'd go into another room to talk, but he didn't mind that either. The girls had splashed most of the water on the floor when he finally said he'd had enough. They dried his feet with the damp towel, then told him to choose a nail polish color. Although he pretended it was a tough decision, he'd known all along he'd choose Candy Apple Red.

"Pedicure time!" Ellen said.

She was off the phone and had put on glasses. They were rectangular with dark frames, and he liked the way they made her look studious.

When she asked him which foot he preferred and then matter-of-factly lifted it onto her lap, her hands were warm, her pants silky, and he worried he'd get hard and she'd know. "My foot is in your hands," he murmured, hoping this was witty, but she was shaking the polish and, suddenly businesslike, didn't respond.

She'd painted about half of his big toenail—he liked the way she took her time and was careful about just how much polish she put on the brush—when the girls started laughing and screaming and running in and out of the room. Ellen practically shoved his foot off her lap so she could go after them. She gave them each a cookie, and they quieted down enough for her to finish his toenail. He wished the experience had been sexier, but he was also relieved because it would be easier to tell Beth. If she couldn't see the humor of the situation and accused him of something like poor judgment, he'd point out she was being sexist.

When Beth got home and Rachel proudly showed off her nails, Jake wondered if she'd tell Beth about his toenail. He hoped she wouldn't. Usually at dinner Beth wanted to hear all the details of Rachel's day, but she seemed tired. Then Rachel spilled her milk.

As soon as everything was cleaned up and Beth took Rachel upstairs to put her to bed, Jake looked for some kind of nail polish remover. When he couldn't find any he took a bath, hoping the warm water might soften things up enough so he could pick off the polish with his fingernail. At first he enjoyed lying in the tub and vowed to do it more often. But when it became clear that the polish wasn't going to come off, he was angry he'd agreed to the pedicure in the first place. He imagined his father, who'd died when Jake was in college, seeing his son's red toenail: he'd be not so much shocked or disapproving as bewildered. Jake felt bewildered, too.

Beth knocked.

"I'm in the tub."

"Can I come in for a minute?"

"Of course." His water had turned cloudy and his toe wasn't visible. He felt furtive. It seemed fitting that he was soaking in his own dirt.

Beth was intent on getting something from the medicine chest and barely looked at him. "You never take a bath!"

"I thought I'd change my routine."

He felt strange, looking up at her. She was wearing black sweatpants and a dark blue sweatshirt.

"I need you to go to the drugstore one of these days," she said. "We're almost out of floss. Enjoy your bath."

She carefully closed the door behind her.

He felt both relieved and, with his red toenail, ridiculous. His water was lukewarm, but he didn't deserve to make it warmer. After a while he got out of the tub. If he slipped and fell, Beth would have to call for an ambulance and everyone would see his stupid painted nail. Rachel's little towel was hanging next to his. It made him sad.

When he went into the bedroom Beth was in her bra

and panties, getting ready for bed. Her closet door was open and he noticed how many dark clothes she had. It seemed funereal.

She was telling him about some new policy at work when she glanced at him—he was naked. "Your toenail!" She flushed. "You let her paint your toenails! Rachel was trying to tell me…I thought she was making it up." She began pacing. "You let her paint your toenails? In front of your daughter?"

His face felt warm and prickly. "One toenail."

"Did you fuck her, too?"

"No, I did not fuck her too." He put on his pajamas. "She did the girls' nails and Rachel kept begging me to do it too. I got the same color she has." He couldn't bring himself to say Candy Apple Red.

"So that's why you were so nasty at Starbucks. And all of a sudden you're taking a bath? At night? Is this some kind of mid-life crisis?"

The phrase irritated him. "It was an activity. It's one nail. Should I have told her my wife wouldn't approve?"

"I'm sure she's heard that line before." She started crying.

Jake felt like crying, too. He remembered how helpless he'd felt in the delivery room when Beth was in pain and there was nothing he could do. "You don't have to worry," he wanted to tell her now. "I wouldn't hurt you—ever." But he realized that sooner or later he was going to have an affair. Somewhere there was a woman who probably didn't even know he existed, and one day she'd be his girlfriend. Just thinking about holding her hand as they wandered on some unfamiliar street was exciting. Just the word girlfriend was exciting. He vowed not to choose someone like Ellen (who probably wasn't interested in him anyway) who Beth—or Rachel—knew. It was all terribly sad. He was sad. But he was also happy.

Beth had put on a short nightgown Jake had always liked. Maybe this was a sign that she wanted to make love.

When they got into bed he moved slightly toward her. She said she'd rather die than have him touch her. She said she was exhausted; she'd never been so tired, ever. After a while, though, she turned to him.

At first their sex was more exciting than usual and he began to hope that somehow, things would work out. They'd go away for a weekend; he'd go clothes shopping with her and urge her to pick something a little brighter—she'd model for him, and he'd get excited; they'd dance in the kitchen like they used to; maybe he'd knock her up again. But after a while their sex was the same as always, and nothing out of the ordinary.

Tar Beach

February. Maggie got to the restaurant half an hour late for her girlfriend Jen's birthday dinner. This was also the night she'd be meeting Jen's eleven year-old daughter.

"I got pooped on by a pigeon," Maggie told them. "Some idiot put bread crusts all over the sidewalk and there were literally dozens of birds swarming all over. It was like pea soup all over my jacket and skirt, and I had to go home to change. Sorry!" She smiled at Ceci, short for Cecelia.

"Pigeons have a right to live," Ceci said angrily. She had big dark eyes and a thin, expressive face. Her tee shirt was from a band Maggie had never heard of. "And people who feed pigeons aren't idiots!"

Jen had warned Maggie that Ceci tended to be jealous of Jen's girlfriends. She was also still mourning her former nanny, Bernadette, who'd died the year before. But Maggie was hopeful: although her experience with children was limited, her college students seemed to like her.

Jen talked about how Maggie loved New York just like Ceci did. (Jen preferred the country.) She talked about how Maggie taught Shakespeare.

"You used to be married to a man?" Ceci asked Maggie.

"I was."

She wasn't going to go into how after almost five not particularly happy years, they'd gone to a couples therapist who'd asked when they'd last laughed together. Neither of them could remember, and that had pretty much been it.

Maggie never had a female lover before. She and Jen had only been dating a few months, but almost immediately she'd felt happier.

Ceci looked at her phone.

Maggie smiled at Jen.

Jen blushed.

Maggie loved it that she blushed. She was glad she'd changed into a dress that showed off her breasts.

Their waiter, in his twenties and darkly attractive, assumed that Maggie was Ceci's mother. They were both thin with curly brown hair. Jen was big-boned and muscular and her short brown hair was straight. Even after Maggie made clear that Jen was the mom, the waiter paid more attention to Maggie. This annoyed her and made her feel protective toward Jen. She was also flattered.

When Ceci went to the bathroom, Jen reached for Maggie's hand. Maggie still wasn't used to being affectionate with a woman in public and felt self-conscious.

"I'm sorry to tell you this, but Bernadette used to feed pigeons," Jen said softly.

"The nanny?"

"Not a big deal," said Jen.

"Shit!"

Before they could discuss it further, Ceci came back.

It took a long time for their food to come. Ceci and Jen had ordered mac and cheese. Since Jen worked with computers, Maggie joked about how Jen loved "all things Mac!"

Ceci made a face as if that was the stupidest thing she'd ever heard. She ate very slowly, talking only to Jen.

Finally the waiter brought cupcakes, one with a lit candle. Ceci barely joined Maggie in singing Happy Birthday. Maggie felt especially awkward since she couldn't carry a tune and Jen had said Ceci had a lovely singing voice.

Jen told the story of how when Ceci first discovered Jen was born in 1980 she'd said, "My God, Mom."

Maggie decided not to say that she'd been born in 1978.

Ceci looked at her phone.

When the meal was over Jen and Ceci went back to their apartment.

For Ceci's sake, Jen wanted to wait a little longer before Maggie would spend the night, and in a way Maggie was relieved. Before Jen, she'd never even imagined herself with a woman. And if she'd thought about it, she would have assumed she'd be with someone who was more glamorous. She also liked big breasts, and Jen's were surprisingly small. That first time, though, as she and Jen stood across from each other in Maggie's study talking about her ailing Mac—Maggie had been the one who abruptly stopped talking, gave her a flirty smile, and said, "Come over here."

They were still getting to know each other. Jen was almost always cheerful, but Maggie was learning she'd had a hard time. Her family still couldn't accept that she was gay. She'd been a mediocre student and dropped out of college. She'd raised Ceci by herself. Maggie didn't want to hurt her.

As soon as Ceci went to bed Jen called to say that the dinner had been fine.

"What did Ceci say?" Maggie felt awkward using her nickname. "You have to tell me." She knew Jen wouldn't lie.

Jen hesitated. "She thinks you're 'kind of judgy.'"

Maggie laughed. "She's probably right."

"I wish you were here," Jen said.

Maggie went to her bedroom and put the phone on speaker.

"What are you doing?" Jen asked.

"Unbuttoning my dress."

As they lay on their beds, Maggie remembered the smell of the hand sanitizer Jen used. Maggie wished she didn't use it right before they ate, but she liked the faint antiseptic smell in bed. She also found it endearing that Jen, who knew so much about technology, preferred plain old phone sex, no Skype.

Maggie's heterosexual friends had been supportive of the relationship, yet Maggie found herself being less open with them about Jen than she'd been about boyfriends. She kept putting off telling her parents. When she was in the elevator of her apartment with Jen, and the head of her Co-op board got on, Maggie was relieved when Jen didn't reach for her hand. She read a novel about a gay woman who said that if her girlfriend had been a horse, she would have loved horses. Maggie wasn't sure she felt that way about Jen. Sometimes she worried she'd been seduced by sad stories from Jen's life the way Desdemona had been wooed by Othello's tales of his war exploits. Sometimes she wondered if she'd end up with a man.

A few weeks after the birthday dinner, Maggie put on a clingy sweater and miniskirt and went to Jen's apartment for the first time. It was a small two-bedroom, two-bath in a big building on Manhattan's Upper East Side. She'd be sleeping over. Jen wore gym shorts and a grey tee shirt, her at-home outfit. Ceci was still at a friend's.

As Jen showed Maggie the apartment, she was embarrassed that there were several waxy Q-Tips on her bathroom sink.

"Didn't your mom teach you to never put anything smaller than your elbow in your ear?" Maggie joked.

Jen reluctantly said they were Ceci's.

Maggie didn't ask why Ceci didn't leave her Q-Tips in her own bathroom.

Ceci had the bigger bedroom. She still had the clown lamp she'd had since she was a child. There was a pile of Archie comics on the floor. On the dresser was a picture of toddler Ceci, her curls even wilder, holding the hand of a slight woman in her fifties with frizzy grey hair.

"Is that Bernadette?" Maggie asked.

Jen nodded.

"She looks nice."

"Um," said Jen, "I have to tell you something."

Maggie was learning that Jen tended to hold things back, especially if they were unpleasant. Maggie's husband had been the same way.

"Remember I told you how Bernadette used to feed the pigeons? Well, since my birthday dinner, Ceci's been saving stale bread and she's been feeding pigeons too." Quickly she added, "She'll get bored with it soon enough."

She opened one of Ceci's dresser drawers and took out a small pile of handkerchiefs.

"Bernadette gave her these."

She held up a white handkerchief with embroidered yellow roses in each corner.

"When Ceci has a cold she brings one of these to school even though the kids tease her."

"I wouldn't have had the courage to do that," Maggie said. She liked Ceci better.

But when Ceci came home—in black leggings, Cardi B tee shirt and high-tops, she looked like a real New York kid—she acted as if Maggie weren't there.

Jen made her say hello, but she was so gentle that Maggie had a feeling she was one of those parents who can't bear to discipline their children.

All through dinner Ceci kept sneaking looks at her phone. When Jen showed them a ceramic teapot a client had made her, Ceci asked if she could be excused.

"Speaking of teapots," Maggie said quickly to Ceci, "when I was probably younger than you I went through this stage of waking up in the middle of the night, worried that a robber would break in and kill me." A psychologist friend had suggested she tell Ceci about her own life instead of just asking about hers, but she wished she'd chosen a better story. "Although he wouldn't really be a murderer, since I was awake and would be able to identify him, he'd have to kill me."

Jen smiled at her encouragingly.

Ceci had her phone on the table in front of her. She kept sliding it around. When it seemed about to fall off, she'd catch it.

"Anyway," Maggie said, "do you know the song, 'I'm a Little Teapot'?"

"I've heard of it," Jen said.

Maggie felt a pang because Jen's childhood lacked so much.

Suddenly Ceci sang "I'm a little teapot, short and

stout," bending one arm like a handle and the other like a spout.

Maggie waited for her to sing the next two lines, but that was it.

"So my plan was, that as soon as the robber saw me in bed I'd sit up and start singing, to the same little teapot tune, 'I am a little blind girl, and I can not hear a thing….'"

Jen laughed. "That's so sweet."

Ceci got up and went to her room. She didn't quite slam the door.

Later, as Maggie and Jen undressed for bed, Maggie said, "Actually, there's more to the teapot song. Ceci just sang the first line." She still felt awkward saying Ceci.

Jen wore the baggy grey tee shirt she wore to bed. On the wall behind her was a framed drawing of a sparkly rainbow unicorn Ceci once made for her.

Jen was sitting on the bed. Maggie put on a sheer white nightgown and stood in front of her.

One arm on her hip and the other bent as if it were a spout, Maggie softly sang about how she was a little teapot, short and stout.

"When I get all steamed up…." Smiling at Jen, she thrust out her chest. "When I get all steamed up," she repeated, huskily this time, "hear me shout." She bent over a little. "'Tip. Me. Over. And. Pour. Me. Out.'"

Jen pulled her onto the bed.

Maggie would say only positive things about Ceci to Jen, but she'd complain to her friends.

"In the summer, mainly to annoy Jen, she goes up to their roof to 'sunbathe'—another wonderful thing Bernadette used to do. I told you about feeding the pigeons, didn't I?"

"My granny used to sunbathe on the roof of her building," a friend exclaimed. "She'd come down covered with soot." She smiled at the memory.

"They used to call it tar beach," another friend said. "Of course, now roofs are painted white and they have swimming pools and barbecues."

Maggie was surprised by how nostalgic her friends sounded.

"Maybe it's petty to bring this up, but another charming thing she does is leave her dirty Q-Tips in Jen's bathroom."

She discovered that several of her friends used Q-Tips to clean their own ears.

"She has her own bathroom," Maggie added. "She could at least leave them there. I'll tell you one thing, when I was her age I never had my own bathroom!"

Later she'd feel guilty for complaining about someone who was still, after all, a child.

May. On a Saturday morning one of Jen's clients had an emergency and Jen had to make a house call. She and Maggie had been planning to take Ceci out to brunch. Maggie offered to take her anyway, but Ceci wouldn't commit. Maggie decided to wait, and at lunchtime Ceci came out of her room.

"I'm hungry!" she said accusingly.

Maggie texted Jen for restaurant suggestions. "I want to take her someplace special. I don't care if it's expensive."

Jen suggested they go to a diner. "She'll be happy and it'll be cheap."

"I like it when you guide me."

She imagined Jen blushing with pleasure.

Although it was overcast and cool, Ceci wore a tee shirt and shorts. She was getting breasts. Her hair really needed to be shaped. Maggie wondered if people would assume they were mother and daughter. She wasn't sure how she felt about that.

They were about to leave when Ceci said, "Wait!" She ran to the kitchen and came back with a bread bag full of crumbs and crusts. Maggie managed not to react.

As soon as they got outside Ceci began emptying the bag near the base of a tree.

An older woman walking by stopped. "How can you let her do that?" she yelled at Maggie, who was trying not to look at Ceci.

Mortified, Maggie didn't respond.

The woman turned to Ceci. "Doesn't your mother tell you that you're attracting vermin?"

"She's not my mom."

The woman gave Maggie a dirty look and walked away.

Maggie wished she could just buy Ceci a hotdog on the street. Or nothing at all. But the sun had come out, and for the first time in weeks it felt like spring. She told herself to stop being so judgy.

At the booth across from theirs in the diner, a beautiful Japanese woman in her twenties with long black hair, wearing something black and silky, was talking intently on her phone. She hadn't touched her hamburger and fries. Maggie was amused because the woman was so delicate looking and the burger was so big.

Ceci was busy with her phone. Jen would have made her put it away, but Maggie appreciated the break from trying to make conversation.

After they'd been eating silently for a while, Ceci said, "Do you think I'm old enough to get my ears pierced?"

Jen had already told Maggie that Ceci was too young. Maggie had been surprised. She would have let her do it.

"I kind of agree with your mom."

Ceci went back to her phone.

The Japanese woman, still on the phone, began crying softly.

"Do you think she's talking to her boyfriend?" Maggie whispered to Ceci.

"How would I know?"

Maggie realized she should have said, "or girlfriend." It hadn't even occurred to her. More and more lately she'd look at women to see if she found them desirable. She definitely liked big breasts. She still looked at men, whatever that meant.

The Japanese woman was leaving. Her long hair hid part of her face, which was pale and wet with tears. She'd barely eaten her burger or her fries.

Maggie thought about how when she told Jen about the lunch, she'd mention the Japanese woman.

"Ceci wasn't at all curious about why she was crying," she'd add.

"Kids that age aren't interested in people watching," Jen would point out.

Maggie realized that was true.

"I was channeling you," she'd tell Jen. "You've taught me so much about kids."

Jen would blush.

One thing Maggie was sure of was that it gave her pleasure to give Jen pleasure.

The Japanese woman's lunch was still there. Suddenly Ceci reached over and grabbed a few fries.

"What are you doing?" Maggie gasped. "You can't just take someone's food like that."

"She left them." Ceci ate a fry. "And I just did it." She ate another. "And you're not my mom."

For the rest of the meal they barely spoke.

Maggie had planned to wait until she and Jen were alone to tell her about the fries, but when they got back to the apartment Jen was there and Ceci told her immediately.

Although Jen scolded her, it was obvious she didn't think it was that bad.

Maggie didn't say anything. As soon as she and Jen were alone, though, she waited—in vain—for Jen to bring up the fries.

"You're too permissive with her," Maggie finally said.

They had their first bad fight.

They made up quickly, but Maggie was becoming more critical of Jen. "You have to read this book," or "You'd love this movie," Jen persisted in telling her, even though they had very different taste. She'd asked Jen several times not to put on hand sanitizer right before they ate, but she kept forgetting. Although Jen regretted having dropped out of college, she seemed unwilling to even try to reapply. Her never wanting to discuss unpleasant subjects, like what she thought Ceci's therapist was doing to earn her enormous fee—was frustrating. And, Maggie wasn't at all sure she wanted Ceci in her life.

When a recently hired, single male colleague asked Maggie out to dinner and she said she was dating a woman, he was obviously intrigued. Maggie let it go, but she was intrigued.

June. Jen was interested in going to a trade show in Philadelphia, but worried about being away for an entire weekend. Maggie offered to stay with Ceci, and Ceci surprisingly agreed.

On Friday Ceci slept over at a friend's and she had plans for most of Saturday. Maggie was relieved, but by late afternoon, when Ceci still hadn't responded to her texts, Maggie went to the apartment.

She rang the bell several times and finally used her key.

Ceci's door was closed.

"Ceci?" Maggie still felt awkward saying her name.

"I'm fine. Leave me alone."

Maggie had brought several books, but she couldn't concentrate. What if Ceci had gotten her ears pierced? At dinnertime she knocked on Ceci's door.

"Do you want mac and cheese?"

"I'm not hungry."

"Is everything okay?"

"It's fine."

"Can I come in?"

"No."

Jen texted to see how things were going. Maggie said everything was fine.

She was loading the dishwasher when she thought she heard Ceci crying. When Ceci didn't respond to her knocking, Maggie opened her door.

Ceci was lying face down on her bed. She wore shorts and a sweatshirt.

"Get out!"

Maggie sat on the edge of her bed.

"I want to help."

"I don't need help."

"Do you want to call your mom?" She realized it was a stupid question.

Ceci sat up. Her eyes were red and puffy. "You know that man who lives down the hall?"

"I don't really know your neighbors." Maggie's heart was pounding.

"His name is Mr. Miller."

"Mr. Miller."

"After I got home I put on my bathing suit and a tee shirt to go up to the roof. He rang the doorbell. He said he had this mail for mom that he got by mistake. Wait a minute."

Under the books and clothes on her bed Ceci found a crumpled envelope. She gave it to Maggie.

It was addressed to Jen and looked like some kind of credit card solicitation.

"He asked me what I was doing and I said I was going to the roof. He said his mom used to sunbathe on their roof. They used to call it tar beach. He said he'd never even been to our roof."

"And?"

"Then he asked if I was wearing a bathing suit under my tee shirt. He asked if he could see it."

Maggie tried to put her arm around Ceci's shoulder.

Ceci pulled away.

"I didn't know what to do. I lifted up my shirt and showed him my suit."

"If you'd been at the beach, he'd have seen your suit.

Everyone would see it. No one would think anything of it. Then what happened?" It was hard for her not to say, Hurry up and get to the part about whether he touched you.

"He said 'nice suit.'"

"That's all?"

"That's all."

"And then?"

"He left."

Ceci started crying. "But then I thought I shouldn't have shown it to him. I should have just closed the door."

"Oh, sweetie," Maggie said. "I would have done the same thing. Everyone would. You didn't do anything wrong. You handled it really well." She sounded like her friends with children who were always telling them, "Good job."

She couldn't wait until Jen got back. As soon as Ceci went to bed they'd ring his doorbell.

"Fuck you, you stupid fuck," they'd scream at him.

He'd say they were a couple of dykes.

Ceci wiped her nose with her hand, then got up and found a handkerchief. Embroidered around the edges were tiny bunches of violets.

Maggie wasn't sure what else to say. Jen would know. But Jen wasn't there.

Maggie just knew she didn't want Ceci to suffer in any way because of what had happened. She just wanted her to be okay. She wanted it so much, it hurt.

You Owe Me One

As Georgia was walking Sam, a friend's dog, he lunged after another dog and Georgia was so startled she dropped the leash. Before she could get it again, Sam ran away. They were on a residential Manhattan street, but there was steady traffic. Georgia was calling "Sam!" and crying when a young man who lived in her building appeared and offered to help. A few minutes later he found Sam sniffing a tree trunk a few blocks away. Georgia, who'd stopped crying, burst into tears of relief.

"I'm so grateful!" she said.

"You owe me one!"

Georgia assumed he was kidding.

His name was Jesse. Although she'd seen him around their building, there were sixteen floors and two elevator lines, and she didn't know anything about him. Skinny, just a little taller than her five feet five, he looked like he was in his mid-twenties. He had a narrow face, dark hair, and wore a pea coat and jeans. Georgia, almost forty, decided there was something feral about him, sexy rather than handsome.

As they walked to their building, she kept stopping to check Sam's leash.

"I have a poodle," Jesse said. "She was my mom's."

Not sure if his mother was alive, Georgia just nodded.

When they got to their lobby—beige modern furniture and ornate chandeliers—he said he lived with his father in the three-bedroom line. Georgia was in a one-bedroom, on the side of the building without a view of the Hudson.

She wondered if she'd seen his father around.

"He's a lawyer, but basically he helps rich people buy art. He travels a lot." Jesse gave her what she thought was an appraising look. "He was a young dad." He bit his thumbnail. "Women always tell me how charming he is."

Georgia touched her curly dark hair, which she wore severely pulled back.

He said he'd dropped out of NYU to work in the music business. Now he was back in school and had an internship writing copy for an ad agency. They'd promised him a full time job when he graduated. He couldn't wait to get his own apartment.

There was something about him that made her feel off-balance.

"Georgia. Tell me. What do you do?"

She said she worked in admissions at a pre-school.

It turned out he'd gone there.

"I probably couldn't get in now. I hear it's become one of those Baby Ivies." He bit his thumbnail again. "Do you have kids of your own?"

"No kids."

"Married?"

"Nope!" She'd stopped telling people that she'd been married, briefly, right after college. "Actually, I should go. I don't know how to thank you. If there's ever anything I can do…."

She waited for him to say how he was happy to have helped.

"We'll see. I'm sure I'll think of something." He gave her a big smile.

A few days later she noticed an attractive man in his early fifties, wearing a leather jacket and expensive-looking boots, going out of the building. If she'd seen him in a different context she wouldn't have noticed a resemblance to Jesse, but it was there, although his hair was a lighter brown and not as long.

"That man who just went out…" she said to the doorman, "does he have a poodle and a son named Jesse?"

"That's him. Ethan."

The next time Georgia saw Jesse he was coming in and she was going out, carrying her late mother's fur coat.

"Nice coat," Jesse said.

"It was my mom's. I don't believe in wearing fur, but she died three years ago and I can't bring myself to just get rid of it." The coat had first belonged to the wealthy daughter of an older man her mother been kind to when he was ill. Although her mother had it altered, Vivienne, the woman's name, was still embroidered across the lining.

"I'm taking it to a tailor to see if he can line my winter coat with it."

"Fur is really sexy," Jesse said. "Don't you know anything?"

Georgia was taken aback. Part of her job was interviewing parents and she prided herself on her ability to read people, but Jesse was confusing. He wasn't exactly flirtatious. Maybe he was gay, although he didn't seem gay.

"Don't forget, you owe me one," he said pleasantly as they parted.

Georgia was running a Q and A for a group of prospective parents before their interviews with the director.

They sat in a classroom in the children's brightly colored seats. Although many parents were wealthy and had a sense of entitlement, the application process made them all anxious. Georgia liked helping people who were under stress. Trying to be informal and non-threatening, she sat on the teacher's table. Her dark dress was demure. She wore pearl earrings and subtle eye make-up; her curls were pulled back into a fancy barrette.

After her PowerPoint presentation, she patiently answered the often repetitious, sometimes irrelevant or aggressive questions that were usually covered in the school catalogue.

"And don't forget to breathe," she joked at the end.

When she went to her office she was surprised and happy to see her colleague Jim, who was on child-care leave and had dropped in to say hello. He was smart and funny and they'd often have coffee or lunch together. He'd been married when they'd met and Georgia liked his wife, too. As they looked at pictures of his baby and Georgia filled him in on gossip, she realized how much she'd missed him.

After he left, she sat at her neat desk and stared into space. Sometimes she worried she'd end up alone like her mother, who'd fallen in love with one unavailable man after another. Georgia had vowed to be different, but she'd married a man who'd turned out to be an alcoholic. She'd gone on to have other relationships that seemed more promising, but nothing lasted. And now here she was, almost forty and still alone. Unlike her single woman friends she wasn't desperate to marry or have a child, but she was lonely. Dreading going back to her neat and orderly—except for her unwashed coffee cup in the sink—apartment, she told herself to breathe. It didn't help.

Over the next few days, as Georgia went in and out of her building she'd catch herself looking for Ethan. But it was Jesse she saw one Saturday, carrying a shopping bag from Saks.

"Where's your mink?" he asked her.

"'Your mink'" annoyed her. "It's still at the tailor's."

He held up the Saks bag. "I bought some clothes for my mom." He explained she'd suffered for years from a neurological disease and now had early dementia.

Georgia could feel herself becoming sympathetic.

"The laundry in her nursing home is always losing her clothes. Or they give her someone else's. My dad gets her stuff in a thrift shop, but I won't do that."

Georgia was touched. Idly she asked where the nursing home was.

"Jersey. It's just across the bridge, but it's sort of a lonely trip." He gave her a shrewd look. "I'm not going to ask you to go with me." He smiled.

He was really preposterous. She remembered how he'd told her how charming his dad was, almost as if he were…pimping for him.

"I've got to go," she said.

"That's okay."

The next time she saw him he was in the lobby with a fancily groomed poodle and a skinny blonde young woman in a tan coat. There was something about the closeness of their bodies that made Georgia think they slept together.

"This is my mom's dog," Jesse said. "Jane." He didn't introduce the blonde.

Georgia decided that even if she met Ethan and they really hit it off, no amount of charm would be worth having such a weird stepson.

When her doorbell rang on a Saturday afternoon without the doorman having called up first she assumed it was her neighbor, an old man who occasionally needed help with his computer.

"It's Jesse."

She partially opened the door.

He wore what looked like a silk shirt and jeans.

"I'm bored, and my dad's home with a date."

Georgia just stood there. It couldn't be easy to see his dad with other women, but she wasn't going to ask him in.

"Can I come in?"

On the other hand, he lived in the building. And he'd found Sam. Even now she couldn't bear to think about how she'd almost lost him. "Just for a minute. I've got work to do."

He sat on the sofa. She sat on a chair across from him. She didn't offer him anything to drink.

He talked about his classes. Georgia half-listened.

"So. Georgia."

He pointed out that the pictures on her wall were too high. He asked about her exercise routine. When she admitted she didn't sweat when she worked out he lectured her about how she was wasting her time. He had a theory that people should touch their toes every day. He went on and on about how bad the food was at a neighborhood restaurant she sort of liked. He couldn't believe she used margarine and not butter.

At one point he shook his head and said, "Don't you

know anything?"

She wondered why she was sitting there listening to this college student scold her. Still, there was something sweet about his shopping at Saks for his mom.

"Did you get your mink back?" he asked her.

She was wary. "Yes."

"Can I see it?"

"You want to see my coat?"

Without waiting for an answer she went to her closet: the sooner she got this over with, the sooner she'd get rid of him.

Her coat was black wool, with shiny black buttons and a round collar. Although she'd had the new lining for a while, it hadn't been cold enough to wear the coat.

She held it so Jesse could see the mink inside.

"Put it on," he said.

"I'm not going to put it on." She showed him the front and the back.

"Put it on."

She just stood there. Still, sooner or later she'd be wearing the coat and she'd run into him, and of course he'd see her in it. And it wasn't as if he were asking her to model lingerie.

"If I do it," she said slyly, "I won't owe you one. My 'debt' will be paid?"

"Yep."

Shaking her head as if she couldn't believe the stupidity of what was happening, she put on her coat. It was closely fitted on the top and then flared out a little. It came to the middle of her knees.

"You missed a button," Jesse said.

She felt irritable like when she was in middle school

and her mother would make her try on winter clothes in August.

"Not bad," Jesse said. "May I?" He got up and walked toward her.

She stepped back.

"I just want to open the top button."

"Why?"

"It'll look better."

"This is so stupid," she muttered, unbuttoning it.

"That's better. Look in the mirror."

"I'm not looking in the mirror."

"I want you to see how sexy you look."

"Thanks so much," she said sarcastically, taking off the coat.

Hanging it up, she realized she could no longer smell her mother's perfume, White Shoulders, a heavy scent her mother would douse herself with every morning. Romantic and sentimental, she'd told Georgia she'd chosen her name so that "one day when your husband takes you to Paris, he'll sing 'Georgia on My Mind' to you on the Champs Elysee." Georgia hated the song, and her own perfume was light and delicate. But she was sad she could no longer smell her mother's White Shoulders.

"Hey! Are you okay?" Jesse asked her.

She'd forgotten he was there. "I'm fine."

"You're sure?"

"Very sure." As soon as he was gone she'd do something relaxing like take a bath. It was still light out, but maybe she'd pour herself a big glass of wine and sip it while she soaked.

"You're sure you're sure?"

"Yes. I also have work to do."

She waited for him to argue, but he shrugged.

After he left she realized that at least her stupid "debt" was paid.

Georgia started wearing her hair loose and got many compliments. She had a few dates with a friend of a friend, but they agreed it wasn't going anywhere. When she didn't see Jesse for several months, she wondered if he'd moved out.

Late one afternoon in the spring, he rang her bell.

She barely opened the door. "What?"

"I'm miserable!"

"Did something happen with your mom?"

"She's the same." He bit his thumbnail. "Can I come in?"

She opened the door, but didn't move.

"What's that noise?" he asked her.

"They're renovating the apartment upstairs."

"It's loud!"

"I know."

"What's your neighbor doing for your pain and suffering?"

She lowered her voice. "Actually, they just sent me a fruit basket."

"That's it?"

She waited for him to lecture her.

"Let's talk in my apartment. It's quieter. My dad's away."

"I have plans," she said, although her friend had cancelled.

"You don't have to stay long."

She'd never seen an apartment in his line and was

vaguely curious. She checked what she was wearing. Black pants and a blue and white striped jersey—neither sexy nor demure.

"Just for a few minutes," she said.

In the elevator she realized she was still wearing her slippers.

The living room, much bigger than hers, had views of the Hudson. Georgia didn't see any photos of Jesse's mom. Ethan probably didn't want his girlfriends to feel inhibited. Georgia wasn't sure if she approved. She sat in what she thought was an Eames chair.

Jesse poured her some of his dad's scotch. She'd never tried single malt. He sat on the floor with Jane.

"You're not drinking anything?" Georgia asked him.

"I don't drink. Not even coffee."

She wondered if he'd had an alcohol or drug problem. She waited for him to tell her his problem, but he just sat there petting Jane. Perfectly groomed, she looked regal. Georgia thought of Jesse's mom, in a room in Jersey, wearing someone else's faded pajamas.

"There's this girl in my statistics class," Jesse said finally.

He showed her Mia's Facebook picture. She was blonde, not the blonde Georgia had seen him with, but also very pretty.

He'd only talked to her twice, briefly, and he couldn't tell what she thought of him. He hoped that another student he'd seen her with a few times wasn't her boyfriend.

"I really like her," he said almost shyly.

Trying not to smile because he sounded so "normal," Georgia gave him the advice she often gave: try to make your own life so satisfying that you'd have to think twice about changing it for anyone.

"It's what I try to do in my own life," she concluded weakly. Lately it hadn't been working very well.

Jesse was rubbing Jane's belly and didn't seem to be listening.

"Georgia, tell me, what music do you like?" he asked her after a while. "Jazz? Frank Sinatra?"

"I just sit around in my mink all day," she said, "listening to the Great American songbook!" She smiled, but she wondered how old he thought she was.

He didn't smile.

"Actually, my mom loved Sinatra," she said. "I mainly listen to podcasts. I should listen to more music." She could feel the scotch. "I'll tell you one song I hate. 'Georgia on My Mind.'" She realized he'd probably never heard of it. She felt old.

"Never heard of it."

"It's about Georgia the state, but it could also be about a woman. Ray Charles sang the most famous version."

"I've heard of Ray Charles."

He took out his phone and played the song.

When it was over, he said, "Not bad."

He went to the bookcase, plugged his phone into the stereo, and played the song again.

Maybe it was the scotch, but it sounded pretty good to her. She couldn't remember the last time she'd heard it. She should have taken her mom to Paris. Her mom had never even been to Europe. Georgia had been there, twice, but she hadn't gone to Paris.

Jesse stood up. When Georgia realized he wanted to dance, she let him pull her up.

As he put his arms around her, Jane barked.

He was a little tentative, as if he weren't used to slow dancing. He didn't have any smell she could identify. Through his silky shirt, his body felt hard and skinny. He drew her closer. Feeling him get hard, she pulled back a little. Neither of them said anything. He kept dancing, and so did she.

Jane was barking again, but the music was so loud that neither Jesse nor Georgia realized Ethan was there. He wore a leather jacket and carried a suitcase and a briefcase.

Jesse and Georgia quickly moved away from each other, and he turned down the volume.

"This is Georgia." He bit his thumbnail.

Ethan gave her a big smile, but she was so embarrassed—the dancing, his scotch, her slippers—she could barely look at him.

He said he'd come back early because he couldn't find some contract. He excused himself to look for it.

"Don't go," he said to Georgia.

She and Jesse just stood there.

"I've got to go!" she whispered, and rushed out.

Back in her apartment, quiet now, she washed the coffee cup she'd left in the sink. Although Ethan was definitely attractive, Georgia doubted they'd be going to Paris. When she saw him—or Jesse—again, she'd smile and keep walking. And that would be that. She felt weirdly happy. It was probably the scotch, but she had to admit it was Jesse, too. His desiring her was flattering and, maybe, just what she needed.

The One Who Makes You Laugh

After Kathy got pregnant and she and Jonathan moved to the suburbs, he stopped going to their Manhattan ophthalmologist, but she kept seeing him. Twelve years later she'd drive their son to the city for his weekly French horn lesson, and since Dr. Meyer's office was nearby it was convenient to schedule her annual appointment. Although she wore glasses for driving and movies, her eyes had always been fine. Still, the exam made her squeamish, and she'd dread the visit.

Gene Meyer's office was in a nondescript white brick apartment building on the Upper East Side. There was something old-fashioned about the practice. His only staff was a middle-aged receptionist Kathy used to mistakenly assume was his wife. The waiting room had faded but comfortable furniture. Dr. Meyer looked around her age—mid-forties, maybe a little older. He had light brown hair, brown eyes, and the frames of his glasses were a yellowish brown. She decided he looked like a Gene, although she wasn't sure what that meant.

"I'm squeamish about eye exams," she reminded him before he started. "I've never actually fainted, but I've come close." She pushed her chin-length dark hair behind her ears. When she talked to men, especially when she said something personal, she was aware of being pretty.

"I'll go slowly," he said, "and explain each step."

"Just get it over with."

Periodically he'd ask how she was doing and she'd

say she was okay. The eye drops stung a little, but she got through it.

His phone rang.

"I have to get this," he told her, and went into the hall.

Sitting there by herself, she wondered if she was depressed. Her son, Noah, had started asking to take the train to the city by himself, and although she knew that was a good sign, it seemed like the beginning of his leaving. Jonathan was more harried since he'd stopped teaching economics and become a dean. She was a writer, mainly stories, but although she'd occasionally get an acceptance from some moderately prestigious journal, her career didn't amount to much.

"I had to take that call," Dr. Meyer said as he came back in. "My wife is dying and I needed to get a refill for her anti-depressant." He sounded matter-of-fact.

"Oh my God, I'm so sorry." She once read something about what you should and shouldn't say to people dealing with life-threatening illness. She couldn't remember anything.

Dr. Meyer went back to examining her eyes.

When he'd ask how she was doing, she'd feel ashamed she'd carried on about her squeamishness.

"Your eyes are about the same," he said when it was over. She was still in the exam chair. He stood beside it.

"I'm so sorry about your wife."

"Diane has breast cancer that had been in remission." He took off his glasses and rubbed the indentations they left on the side of his nose. "It's just the two of us. We've always been close."

"How long have you been married?" she asked softly.

"Twenty-four years. We'd be happy to eat out or go

to a museum or a play with just each other. If we were supposed to go out with another couple and they couldn't make it, we'd almost be glad." He stared into space. "Anyway," he shrugged, "I have another patient."

"I'm so sorry," Kathy said again, and left. She'd looked forward to having the exam over with. Now all she could think about was how the next time she saw him, his wife would probably be dead.

She'd planned to meet Noah near where she'd parked the car, but it was unusually warm for October and when she saw an empty table outside a small café, she texted him to meet her there. Although she yearned for a glass of wine, her eyes were still blurry. She'd also have to drive home. She ordered coffee.

It was twilight, and the street looked romantic and alluring. It made her remember her twenties when she'd lived across town in a tiny studio, dated what seemed like one inappropriate man after the other, and was unhappily in grad school. When she'd sometimes get nostalgic Jonathan would ask her how she could miss a time when she was so unhappy. She didn't know.

As soon as she saw Noah—his thick brown hair, his slouching, skinny body—she felt better.

"How was your lesson?" she asked him.

"Fine."

More and more lately, that had become his typical response. She missed the little boy who'd chatter to her for hours. But so far he did all right in school and seemed okay. After threatening to quit the French horn, he'd surprised them by agreeing to try music school in the city.

"You know what?" Kathy said. "I know you have homework, but let's do something different."

He looked wary. Like Jonathan, he didn't like surprises.

"Let's have dinner right here. We won't be home too late, and Daddy will be fine without us." She'd order something she'd usually deny herself, like a cheeseburger.

"I want to go home," Noah said. He'd never really liked the city.

Kathy drank her coffee quickly.

Walking to the car, Noah let her hold his hand.

He kept in his earbuds the whole ride home. She couldn't stop thinking about Gene Meyer and Diane and how sad life can be.

At dinner she wondered if Noah would nag Jonathan about taking the train to the city by himself (she'd been evasive). He didn't. Jonathan talked about the latest crisis at work. A poet had come from California to be the college's poet in residence for the year, but after a few weeks he announced that the East wasn't for him, and quit.

"I'll tell you one thing," Jonathan said, "from now on I'll consider it my mission in life to bad-mouth him to anyone I meet who likes his poetry."

He and Noah argued about whether the designated hitter was good for baseball. Jonathan pretended to be more interested in the subject than Kathy knew he really was. She missed the stubble he'd had before joining the administration, but he looked good in the more-expensive clothes he now bought.

She decided not to bring up Dr. Meyer's wife.

After dinner Noah did his homework and Jonathan worked in his study. To cheer herself up, Kathy started watching a new special by one of her favorite stand-up comedians.

After a while she realized that Jonathan was standing in the doorway.

"I can hear you laughing," he said.

"I'll close the door."

"It's not that."

She'd paused the show when he came in. He was more critical than she was, and except for The Sopranos—he'd periodically re-watch the whole series—he rarely watched television.

"I want to be the one to make you laugh," he said. He was still in the doorway.

Briefly she wondered if he was kidding, because she'd never thought of him as being particularly funny.

"Aren't I funny, too?" he asked her.

"You can be funny." She wished he'd come into the room so she didn't have to turn around to see him. "Remember that time we gave Noah a sip of champagne and you said it was a statutory grape?"

"That was years ago. He was a toddler."

"And the time you said that all European men look gay to you, and then you said not to tell that at your memorial because then no one would miss you?"

"It's like you have to think of examples. Am I that pathetic?"

She took off her glasses. "I didn't mean it like that." She tried to think of a boyfriend who'd made her laugh. Paul, who she'd dated in her twenties, could be funny. He'd also suffered from depression. Actually, he was funniest when he was depressed. Something else that was sad.

"Do I make you laugh?" she asked Jonathan.

"Sometimes."

He kept standing in the doorway. She put on her

glasses and started watching again. The comic was telling a long story about oral sex. He said Fuck a lot. Jonathan rarely cursed. It was unsettling to have him there.

When she turned around, he was gone.

Getting ready for bed, she wondered if the comic made his girlfriends laugh. Maybe they complained he saved it all for his work. She wondered if Dr. Meyer made his wife laugh. He didn't seem like he'd be funny, but maybe when he wasn't giving eye exams he was. Kathy sighed. She could hear Jonathan on the phone in his study, complaining about the poet who'd just up and left.

The next day Kathy went to see her new friend Beth, who'd recently moved from Chicago with her husband, a neurosurgeon, and their toddler daughter Sonia. A former actress, Beth had long black hair, wore a lot of eye make-up, and had a way of leaning toward Kathy when they talked that was almost flirtatious. She was six years younger, and although Kathy's other mom friends were closer to her own age, the women had immediately liked each other.

They sat in Beth's messy kitchen drinking coffee while Sonia, in her highchair, ate lunch and occasionally threw pieces of carrot and chicken on the floor.

Kathy told Beth what Jonathan had said about making her laugh.

"The thing is, if he hadn't brought it up I wouldn't be particularly aware of it. Now I wonder, I don't know, if something is missing." She thought about how he made it possible for her to write full time, and never complained that she made no money. She pushed her hair behind her ears. "Does Gary make you laugh?"

"Occasionally." When Beth talked about her husband she'd sound bitter because after pressuring her to have a child, he was always at work.

"Anyway, Jonathan's not not funny," Kathy said.

"Ed was funny," Beth said. He was a married rabbi she'd had an affair with in Chicago. "But what I really miss is the sex." She started crying.

Kathy couldn't remember crying that way over a lover.

Seeing her mother crying, Sonia burst into tears.

When both of them had calmed down Kathy said, "I almost forgot!" She told Beth about Gene Mayer's wife.

"Their relationship sounded so romantic. It's heartbreaking."

"Hmmm," said Beth.

"Why 'Hmmm'?"

"It's just that if you end up sleeping with him, it's going to be tricky. I mean, his wife isn't even dead yet."

Kathy was shocked she'd even think such a thing.

Later it occurred to her that although their recent conversation had been painful, Beth usually made her laugh.

After Jonathan found a poet to fill in for the one who'd left, he and Kathy went out for a celebratory drink.

A local hotel had recently renovated their lounge with reupholstered furniture and a new sofa. Kathy and Jonathan were sitting by the gas fireplace drinking champagne and eating stuffed clams when a woman whose child used to be in Noah's class came in with a man Kathy didn't know.

"Kathy?" the woman said. "Maya. Ariella's mom?"

Although Maya wasn't particularly pretty, she wore an expensive-looking black dress and looked good. Kathy wished she weren't wearing jeans and sneakers. Maya introduced her companion, Michael, as an old friend. He wore a baseball cap, a look Kathy usually disliked, but she found him boyishly handsome. After the women made small talk about their children's schools, Maya and Michael sat on the sofa across the room.

Jonathan complained about a new personnel problem at work. He complained a lot more than when he was teaching. Kathy kept sneaking looks at Maya and Michael. They weren't sitting particularly close to each other, but there was something about the intense way they were talking that made Kathy wonder if they were having an affair.

"Are you okay?" Jonathan asked.

"What do you mean?"

"I don't know," Jonathan said. "Lately you seem kind of…remote."

"I'm fine. Really. Don't I seem fine?"

"I guess."

Maya had finished her wine. Occasionally she'd touch Michael's arm. He leaned close, but never touched her.

Kathy decided they'd been lovers years before, but then Maya met the man she'd marry and ended it. Now, although she was still married, she wanted to resume their affair. But he'd met someone else and, although he still loved Maya, he wanted to give the other woman a chance. Kathy realized it sounded like a story, although not the kind she wrote.

The next time Jonathan watched The Sopranos, Kathy joined him. Although she'd enjoyed it when it first came out she disliked the violence, and when he'd suggest they re-watch an episode, she usually said no.

They watched one where one of the more appealing characters is murdered.

Kathy rested her legs on his lap, and he warmed her cold feet in his warm hands.

Because Jonathan tended to be so critical, they had an agreement that when they saw a play or movie, he'd wait to see if she liked it before saying something negative. Almost always, though, she could tell.

"It's still good," he said when the episode was over. "You know, people think that if you're critical, you like feeling superior. But that isn't true. I'm happy when I really enjoy something."

He said it every time.

"Are those new glasses?" he asked her as she took them off.

"No. Why?"

"No reason."

"Don't you like them?"

"They're okay. I mean, they're fine."

They talked about weekend plans. She mentioned they'd be having dinner with Beth and Gary.

"Actually," he said, "I'm not that crazy about Beth."

"Really? Why?"

"I'm not sure." He shrugged. "You seem sort of distant," he said suddenly. "I miss you."

She touched his arm. "I'm here."

"I only miss you when you're here."

She stopped herself from saying, "See, you can be funny."

In June, Kathy googled Diane Meyer and saw that she'd died in May. She learned that Diane was from

Cleveland, taught third grade, and volunteered for various cultural institutions. She was five years older than Kathy. There was no picture. Kathy began several sympathy notes to Dr. Meyer. She didn't like any of them.

The mother of a student Noah had become friendly with in music school invited him for dinner after the last class. Jonathan and Kathy decided she'd drive him in as usual, and then let him take the train home by himself. After Kathy dropped him off, on an impulse she decided to stop by Dr. Meyer's office on the chance that he'd be between patients long enough for her to offer her sympathy.

His receptionist had left, and he came to the waiting room. He looked the same, maybe a little thinner.

"I'm sorry I barged in. I wanted to tell you how sorry I am about your wife. I should have just written a note."

He seemed confused. "I'm expecting a patient, but she's the last of the day. Can you wait? Maybe go out and come back in half an hour?"

Kathy wished she'd just written a note, but felt that now she had to wait.

For a few minutes she stood in the lobby and tried to guess which of the women going in was his patient. It was interesting how many people looked as if they were about to have an eye exam. A very pretty woman smelling of expensive perfume came in. Kathy was sure she was Dr. Mayer's next patient until the woman started looking for something in her purse and then, as if she lived in the building, took out a set of keys. Kathy went outside. The day had been cloudy, but now, in late afternoon, the sun had come out. She decided that as soon as she was through with Dr. Meyer, instead of going home she'd meet a friend for dinner. She made a few calls, and although it turned out that no one was available, she texted Jonathan to pick up Noah.

"Maybe I'll take myself out to dinner in the city."

He seemed pleased she'd be giving herself a treat.

She walked around the block a few times, and when she went back to Dr. Meyer's office he came right out. He'd taken off his white coat and wore a tan dress shirt. He led Kathy into his office.

The room was on the small side, but sunlight poured in from the casement windows. Dr. Meyer sat at his desk, and she sat in one of the two chairs in front of it. There was a small picture of Diane: thin, with short dark hair, she was standing beside a tree and smiling. There was something about her that reminded Kathy of herself.

Dr. Meyer took off his glasses and rubbed his eyes.

"I'd offer you a drink," he said, "but I have nothing here."

Suddenly she really wanted a drink.

"Why am I sitting so far way?" Dr. Meyer said. He got up and moved to the chair next to her.

She'd been physically closer to him when he examined her eyes, but this felt different. She wondered uneasily if he was going to make a pass. Grief could make people do strange things.

But he began talking about what a good teacher Diane had been. Then he talked about how compassionate the hospice nurses were.

"I'm talking too much," he said.

Kathy shook her head. She was touched by his loneliness. He seemed so sad, she wanted to make him laugh. There was something almost seductive about the fact he'd literally looked more deeply into her eyes than anyone else ever had. If he asked her to have dinner with him on this one night when she just happened to be free—she wouldn't say no.

"You know, one of the last things Diane and I discussed—not that long ago, really—was whether it would make sense for me to reconfigure the waiting room and rent the extra space to an optician." Dr. Meyer went over the pros and cons of the plan in some detail.

Kathy's face felt stiff from trying to look interested. She couldn't wait to get out of there.

When he finally stopped talking, she got up and, as if she'd just realized the time, said she had to pick up her son.

Dr. Meyer walked her to the door. He sighed, thanked her, and said he'd see her in a few months.

It occurred to her that maybe it was time to get another ophthalmologist, someone more local. Jonathan seemed to like his.

She called another friend, but she had dinner plans. Without really thinking about it Kathy drove back to Westchester.

But she didn't feel like going home. Even though Noah wouldn't be there for another hour, she parked at the station. Cars were pulling up to meet the train from New York. Kathy pretended not to see two people she knew. Soon everyone drove away, and people started to gather for the next train into the city. Jonathan had probably eaten. She could go by herself to her favorite local restaurant. It was strange: if anyone she knew saw her eating there by herself, they'd assume Jonathan was away. She could take the train back to the city and have dinner in her old neighborhood. That would be stupid. No one knew where she was. She kind of liked that. She was getting really hungry.

The Super's Son

Early Spring

When Suzanne rang the super's bell to pick up a package—his widow, Carmen, still lived there—Carmen's son opened the door. In his mid-twenties, Eddie was tall and thin, with dark eyes and black hair. Although it was still cool, he wore cutoff jeans and a tee shirt. He looked as if he worked out. Every time Suzanne saw him she'd think that he was really very attractive.

He looked at her belly pushing out her flowered maternity dress—four months pregnant, she was so thin and small-boned, she'd started to show almost immediately—and gave it a thumbs-up.

Suzanne asked about his young son.

"He's great!" Eddie looked happy at the thought of him. "He's in the Bronx with his mom. I'm back home for a while." They all lived in a small apartment building on Manhattan's Upper West Side.

Suzanne was pretty sure he went to college, at least part-time. "How's school?"

"Good. I want to teach history one day, hopefully in a middle school."

"I used to teach high school. English." She didn't say she'd hated it and, with her husband Marc's encouragement, had recently quit.

"I'm also working nights as a waiter. You have a package, Suzanne? I'll get it."

She'd always been pleased that unlike Carmen, Eddie called the tenants by their first names. As she waited she thought about how their apartment often smelled as if Carmen were cooking something delicious. Now it was garlic and a spice she couldn't identify. She felt a little light-headed and realized she hadn't eaten lunch.

Eddie came back with a package. Marc must have ordered shoes. As Suzanne took the box, it slipped out of her hands, and the next thing she knew she was stretched out on a large sofa and Eddie was bending over her looking worried.

"Are you okay?"

"I'm okay." His face was close to hers, and she wanted him to barely touch her nipples, then lift up her dress, pull down her panties—she'd help.

She sat up. "I'm fine."

He still seemed worried. "I'm gonna get you some juice."

She told herself that Eddie couldn't have been aware of her desire for him.

She hoped she didn't look too bad. She touched her thick curls, which got limp and lusterless when she was sick. They felt all right. Her hormones must be all over the place. She and Marc hadn't had sex as often as they used to, mainly because he seemed inhibited as if, despite her assurances, he could somehow hurt the baby.

She looked around. The apartment faced the back and didn't get much light, but the living room was large with high ceilings. There were several tables and large, comfortable-looking chairs. Music played somewhere, so softly that she couldn't tell if the words were Spanish. She saw a small bowl filled with hard candy on the coffee table and was about to take a piece when Eddie came back with a glass of orange juice and a plate of Saltines.

"Here you go, Suzanne." As she ate the crackers and drank, he didn't take his eyes off her.

"I don't know what happened. I usually snack all day long." She stood up. "I'm really fine."

He'd reached to help her, but she'd been too quick. He insisted on accompanying her upstairs.

An electrician was high up on a ladder in the middle of the lobby, fixing a chandelier. As she and Eddie waited for the elevator, they didn't speak. She was glad none of her neighbors was going in or out of the building. Eddie was holding Marc's package—she'd forgotten about it.

In the elevator she couldn't think of anything to say. She looked at his black sneakers. Apparently Eddie couldn't think of anything to say either. It was like the end of an awkward date.

When they got to her apartment she murmured, "Thank you so much!" She was about to open her door when Eddie said, "Not so fast, Suzanne!"

She froze.

He handed her Marc's shoes.

Marc had chosen estates law because it was less pressured than litigation, but he rarely got home before eight o'clock. Suzanne usually enjoyed those early evening hours waiting for him. She'd eat popcorn or pretzels and make herself a decaf coffee, instant and in a glass the way her mom did it, even though she and Marc had a Nespresso machine. She'd lie on the velvet chaise longue which Ben and Ruthie, Marc's parents, had given them. Sometimes she'd read. She was trying to finish the first volume of

Remembrance of Thing Past before the baby came. Marc recently bought her an expensive camera, and she was still studying the manual. Tonight, though, feeling vaguely that she didn't deserve the chaise, she sat on a chair. She couldn't concentrate on Proust, and didn't even try the manual. She'd had lovers who would have found it sexy if she told them what had happened with Eddie, but Marc wasn't like that.

When they'd started dating he fell in love with her almost right away, but she wasn't so sure. He was preoccupied with his job, complained a lot, and was an alarmist about health issues. His intensity could get on her nerves. He listened to talk shows on the radio in every room he was in; it seemed like there was always noise when he was around. "I need you!" he'd tell her, and although she didn't quite see why he was so needy—he came from a loving family and had a successful career—she came to enjoy making him happy. And then slowly, for her, she fell in love with him. But even after they were married, she'd sometimes have doubts. After he was made a partner he'd sworn he'd cut down on his weekend hours and for a while he did, but soon he was back to his old ways. When she couldn't get pregnant she'd thought about leaving. Then she had fertility treatments, got pregnant and, perhaps because they'd gone through so much worry together, her doubts seemed to disappear.

Uncomfortable in the chair, she wondered if she was old enough to be Eddie's mom; if he was, say, twenty-three, she would have had to have him when she was twelve. She thought about calling a friend and telling her what had happened, but she didn't move. She wasn't even sure she'd tell Marc about fainting: he'd just worry. Wondering if she'd felt the baby kick or it was just gas, she fell asleep.

Then Marc was there, turning on lights all over the apartment the way he always did, muttering, "Why is it so dark in here?" It was their routine: she'd wait for him with just one light on, in the room where she was; he'd tease her for being "small change"; she'd feel—especially since she'd stopped teaching—that he was bringing her the world.

"I must have fallen asleep." She shielded her eyes from the light.

"Is everything OK?" He fingered the place on his head where his new hairdresser had predicted he'd have a bald spot one day. Although the dermatologist he'd consulted afterwards hadn't been able to see it, and neither had Suzanne, he believed the hairdresser.

"Everything's fine. Your shoes came." She remembered Eddie's black sneakers.

As she got the dinner ready, she could hear a woman's voice on the radio in their bedroom. Stirring soup, she missed her wooden spoon, which she'd bought for her first apartment. Marc had decided it was unsanitary.

"You have a responsibility for the baby now," he'd said.

"You really think I'm going to get germs from a spoon that will be powerful enough to hurt the baby?"

He didn't really answer, but she stopped using the spoon.

Suddenly annoyed because she couldn't tell him about fainting, she was tempted to look for it. "The wooden spoon rebellion!" she thought bitterly. But even if Marc came in while she was using it, he'd probably be too preoccupied with some problem at work to notice.

They ate at their big dining room table.

"Soon we'll have a little person joining us." The thought cheered her up. "Does this soup seem salty?"

"Not particularly."

"I bought it at this new place your mom told me about." Ruthie was always recommending take-out that Suzanne usually found too salty.

As Marc complained about a demanding client, Suzanne was bored but reminded herself that he worked hard so that she—and soon their baby—wouldn't have to "think about," as he put it, money.

She'd roasted a chicken and made a salad. He ate quickly.

"Slow down."

He took a deep breath. "That's better!" But soon he was doing it again.

While she loaded the dishwasher he came in to tell her something stupid one of his partners had said. In the middle of his story he abruptly stopped, as if he knew he was being tedious. He could do that sometimes, and she found it endearing.

His mother called—Suzanne could always tell who it was because he'd sound relaxed. Suzanne had always liked Ruthie, and now she was grateful because Ruthie and Ben had paid for her fertility treatments.

When Marc hung up he asked if she wanted to call her mother, who lived in Cleveland.

"Not tonight." Her mother cried a lot, not only when she was sad or moved by something, but when, say, someone tried to get ahead of her in line or she wanted to return something to a store. Susanne's father had died young and Suzanne had felt close to and protective of her mother until, in her teens, she'd grown impatient. Marc would tell Suzanne she was too hard on her. Sometimes this annoyed her, but it also pleased her that he really seemed to care about her mother.

As if he sensed Suzanne's having been attracted to another man, he wanted to make love, even though it was what he called a "school night"—he had work the next day.

For a change she wasn't in the mood. She let him assume it was because of her pregnancy.

He kissed her cheek and turned on his bedside radio.

"You know," she hesitated, "I'm not sure I'm really a photographer." She'd always enjoyed taking pictures, but with a simple camera and then with her smart phone; before Marc encouraged her, she'd never thought of doing it full time. "And it was one thing to take pictures when I was working, but now I feel guilty that's all I do." Growing up, she'd always had some sort of job.

"Being a photographer isn't work?"

"I haven't even really learned to use the camera yet…."

"Give yourself time." He was almost asleep.

She turned off the radio, got up, and went into what would be the baby's room. Rocking in the antique rocker Ruthie had bought them, she wondered if Eddie had carried her to the couch. He obviously worked out, but wasn't too muscular. She worried her skin had felt clammy. Eventually she fell asleep. Toward morning Marc came looking for her and led her back to their bed.

Early Summer

Although Suzanne was often in and out of her building and would occasionally see Carmen—short, overweight, polite but reserved—cleaning the lobby or hallways, she rarely saw Eddie. Once she was coming into the lobby with a grocery bag when he opened his apartment door and looked pleased to see her.

"Let me take that up for you," he said.

"It's really light. How's school?"

"School's good."

"How's work?"

"Work's work." He smiled. "How's baby?"

She realized her hand was on her stomach. "Nine more weeks." She couldn't think of anything else to say. She had a feeling he wasn't usually so reticent, either, especially with women. She couldn't tell if he found her attractive.

Another night she was coming in with Marc as Eddie was going out. "How's it going?" Eddie asked without slowing down.

Marc nodded in his usual preoccupied way.

"He's a nice young man," Suzanne said as soon as the elevator door closed.

"He seems to be."

She could tell he was thinking about work.

A few days later, near the playground across from their building, she saw Eddie with his three or four year-old son, who had bangs and wore a Yankees cap. Eddie didn't see her. She took their picture, and although she was often critical of her photos, she liked it and—without any note—put it under Carmen's door.

In early July she was waiting for the elevator when Eddie came in the building. She wore a flowery jersey dress. Eddie looked at her basketball-like belly and sort of saluted it. They talked about the heat.

"How's school?"

"Since you asked, when I decided to do this thing I told myself that I'd get all A's. But I just got a B."

"I seem to remember getting a few C's." She couldn't believe she'd said, "seem to remember"—like some little old lady.

"Anyway, I'm going to have to work more hours anyway. I'll probably take off the fall semester and go back in the spring."

She wasn't sure what to say. Then the elevator was there.

"See you, Suzanne. Take care."

"See you." She felt shy about saying his name.

Occasionally she'd hear him in the small courtyard behind their building, playing ball with his son. She'd wonder if Marc would find the time to play ball with their child. He said he enjoyed tennis, but he never played.

Every time she and Marc approached whatever restaurant they were going to, she'd worry that Eddie worked there—she didn't want him to wait on them.

When Marc left a shirt with a fraying collar on top of their garbage so one of the workmen in the building could see if he wanted it, Suzanne worried Eddie would take it and she'd hate seeing him wear it. She was about to stuff it in the garbage when she remembered how much taller and thinner Eddie was. He also probably wouldn't be caught dead in Marc's dress shirt.

She'd catch herself having fantasies about him. They'd be in the elevator and it would be packed to capacity (this had never happened): Eddie would be pressed against her belly, baby would give a big kick, and Eddie would laugh; the other tenants would look at him inquiringly, but it would be his and Suzanne's secret. He'd be patiently listening to a woman in the building complain about some problem in her apartment when Suzanne, passing by, would inform her that Eddie had schoolwork to do. (The woman would never speak to her again.) Marc would be at work when she went into labor, and she'd be hailing a cab to take her to the hospital when Eddie would come out of their building: he'd insist on going with her and waiting until Marc got there; the next time Marc saw him he'd try to give him a big tip, but Eddie would angrily refuse to take it. Leaving the baby with a sitter, Suzanne would be on her way out when she'd see Eddie, and as they made small talk her milk would let down, soaking her shirt—and he'd notice. What if she needed drugs in the delivery room and after they gave her something she babbled to Marc (and to the doctors and nurses who were there) about how she'd been dying to have Eddie fuck her?

She more or less mastered her new camera, but didn't take many pictures. She liked to photograph people, and while it had been easy to hide what she was doing with her smart phone, now her subjects were aware of her big camera and usually didn't like it. Marc explained her legal rights, but when someone objected she'd sympathize. On hot days the camera strap, damp with her sweat, irritated her neck. More and more, instead of taking pictures she'd just walk in the park. When it was too hot to walk, or raining, she'd go out for coffee or lunch or to an afternoon movie, usually alone since most of her friends had jobs. Or she'd lie on her chaise with the air conditioner blasting and feel guilty because Marc worked so hard and even her mom, in her sixties, was a full-time secretary. Sometimes she'd worry about what kind of job she'd get when her baby went off to school.

It was a strange time with Marc. Although by unspoken agreement they had sex less often, they were closer. When she got home after taking or not taking pictures, she'd put on his gym clothes, which now fit her. The wait for him seemed longer and lonelier. After dinner they'd sit side by side on the sofa and he'd keep his hand on her belly, patiently (for him) waiting for the baby to move. He kept telling her how grateful he was that she'd persuaded him not to find out the baby's sex. He quickly mastered her camera and took arty pictures of her naked.

One night as they lay in bed talking, he told her about the summer when he was interning in Washington and had an affair with another intern "who happened to be black."

Suzanne was surprised he'd never told her. "Was she pretty?"

"She was. She was a little taller than me and skinnier than you, and her hair was like those halos on angels in medieval paintings. Anyway, it turned out she had a boyfriend in Florida and it didn't last long. Are you shocked?"

"No. Maybe a little surprised." She smiled.

He looked pleased with himself.

"Do you think you would have ended it if she hadn't?"

"I can't answer that."

"Don't talk like a lawyer."

"Who should I talk like?" He sounded almost wistful.

It was a school night for him and getting late, but they made love.

Another night she talked about her first love, Steve. Although Marc knew that he was probably an alcoholic, she'd never told him about how, after she'd left him, he'd been in a car accident that was probably his fault. "He kept calling from the hospital, but after I found out it wasn't serious I didn't want to go see him. He kept begging and finally I went." She tried not to cry. "He looked grizzled and grey. The worst thing…" she felt the tears come, "the worst thing was that one of his eyelids no longer stayed closed, so at night—to this day—he has to use this special tape to keep it shut." She covered her face with her hands, partly because she was crying, but she also had a feeling that Marc would look squeamish, and she didn't want to see that.

Several weeks went by without her running into Eddie. Once she came home to find he must have left a large package for Marc outside their door. Then a neighbor told her that Carmen had breast cancer and needed chemo. Eager to ask if there was anything she could do to help, Suzanne began lingering in the lobby, slowly going through her mail or prolonging small talk with neighbors, but she didn't see Carmen or Eddie.

Marc was late for their childbirth class so Suzanne was paired with Linda, a single parent who usually worked with the instructor. As they practiced massage techniques on each other Suzanne liked the feel of Linda's hands, smaller than Marc's, but more confident. And she liked massaging Linda's body and trying to ease its tension. When Marc rushed in, shrugging off his expensive suit jacket, Suzanne was disappointed.

After class they usually had dinner at a nearby restaurant that happened to be the same one where, before Suzanne had even met Marc, she'd taken her mother for her birthday. She'd budgeted for weeks to afford it. Her mother, her dyed black hair too vibrant for her pale face, had been so excited and grateful that she'd cried even more than usual. Diners at nearby tables didn't seem to notice, but Suzanne was embarrassed. Now when she'd go with Marc she'd remember that night and feel disoriented. Since the class met on a school night, Marc always tried to choose a dish that wouldn't take too long. Although Suzanne wouldn't say anything, it bothered her to spend so much on a meal they rushed.

When they got outside she saw a Cuban-Chinese restaurant a few doors down. "Let's go somewhere else for a change," she said. "Let's go there!" She expected him to object because it looked humbler than their usual choices, but he agreed.

As they walked in Suzanne realized this was the first restaurant she'd been to where Eddie could conceivably be a customer and not a waiter. As far as she could see, he wasn't there.

The booths were large and the padded leather benches were comfortable. There was a table of attractive young women all sipping pink drinks from big cocktail glasses with little umbrellas in them. Suzanne wished she weren't pregnant and could have a glass of wine. When their waiter asked Marc if he wanted white or yellow rice, Marc looked at Suzanne. "Which one do I like?"

She shrugged. She no longer found questions like that endearing.

He ordered a diet Coke. This used to depress her, but since she'd been pregnant she'd gotten to like them, too.

There was a lot of food. They talked about ways they'd be like and unlike their friends who had children. As Suzanne swore she wasn't going to get a jogging stroller—"When I'm with my baby, I'm going to be with my baby!"—she had a feeling from Marc's expression that his parents had already bought them one. She remembered the night when they were on their honeymoon in Paris and the concierge had given them a gift certificate from his parents to a three-star Michelin restaurant. The meal was the best she'd ever had, but there was something about the whole thing that had made Suzanne uncomfortable. She vowed she wasn't going to take hundreds of baby pictures.

Marc promised to get home earlier. "I know you don't believe me, but you'll see." He'd finished eating and was jiggling his foot. When she first met him she'd thought that meant he was madly attracted to her.

"Give me a minute." He took out his phone and called a young associate who'd been doing research for him.

Suzanne decided to call her mother.

She sounded teary with happiness at hearing Suzanne's voice. "Five more weeks and then you'll have this wonderful new person in your life…."

Suzanne felt guilty for no longer being in her mother's life. "Marc said you're going to be the first one he calls," Suzanne said. "By the way, has Martha's son put away those boxes yet?"

Martha had multiple sclerosis, and Suzanne's mother had moved into her house the year before. In exchange for free rent, she was there at night in case Martha needed help. Her mother liked Martha, and her room was big and sunny. But in one corner there was still a pile of Martha's boxes that her son kept promising to move to the attic.

"If you don't want to ask him," Suzanne said, "I can make an excuse to call him, and then I'll casually mention it."

"They bother you more than me."

Their waiter appeared and Marc, still on the phone, scribbled in the air to indicate he was ready for the check.

"Gotta go, mom." Putting away her phone, Suzanne felt guilty for not talking longer.

When the check came Marc was impressed by how cheap the meal had been. "The food's pretty good, too," he said.

"Rice and beans. It's comfort food." She patted her belly. "Would you come back?"

He smiled. "Probably not." He touched the place where he worried his bald spot would be.

She realized that when the baby came he'd get home early for a week or two, and then he'd be later and later. And then when he finally came, he'd worry about every little thing with the baby. It would be like she had two babies. She wondered if she loved him. She loved her mother, but she could barely stand to talk to her. She knew one thing: she'd love her baby.

Early Fall

Marc's parents had a big end of summer party on the roof of their apartment building. They'd hired a waiter, a bald young man who resembled Eddie. As Suzanne watched him circulate with his big tray of hors d'oeuvres, she saw that it was Eddie. At first she was upset because he was less attractive without his hair, but when she realized that he must have shaved his head for Carmen, who was losing her hair from chemo, she was moved.

He came over to her and held out his tray, but she didn't look at it. Gesturing toward his head, "Nice!" she murmured. "You did it for your mom?"

"Sort of."

"That's so nice of you!"

He shrugged.

"How's she doing?"

"She's feeling pretty good. The chemo hasn't been as bad as we thought. How about you, Suzanne?" Instead of indicating her belly as he usually did, he looked into her eyes. "Pretty soon now, right, Mami?"

Ruthie came up to them, with Marc's younger sister, Greta, in from Chicago.

"Are those miniature lobster rolls?" Greta asked as she took two.

Ruthie said she'd sampled too many.

Eddie again held out the tray to Suzanne, but she shook her head—she didn't want him to wait on her—and he moved on.

She decided not to tell Ruthie and Greta why Eddie was bald. She didn't want it to be party chitchat.

Ruthie, a psychologist, wore a lot of bright colors and was so vivacious she seemed better looking than she was. Greta had very black hair, wore a lot of eye make-up, and was very pretty.

"I can't believe you convinced my brother not to find out the baby's sex."

Ruthie shook her head slowly to show her amazement.

Suzanne felt proud of herself. "For a while he worried he wouldn't be able to stand the suspense so he was going to find out and not tell me, but then he changed his mind."

Ruthie liked to tell Suzanne "Little Marc" stories.

"This was when he was about five," she said. "We'd taken the kids to Coney Island—Greta wasn't even walking yet—and we were on our way to Nathan's when Little Marc saw a dwarf on the boardwalk. He was just standing there smoking a cigarette, but Marc got so deathly pale I thought he was going to faint. After we explained what a dwarf was, he didn't say anything for a few minutes. Then he announced, 'I'm not a dwarf!'"

Suzanne sometimes thought that in some of Ruthie's stories Little Marc wasn't very appealing, but she liked this one.

Ruthie went to greet a friend. As Suzanne chatted with Greta about her latest boyfriend, the baby started moving. "Do you want to feel?" She put Greta's hand on her belly.

Greta was thrilled. "Did my mom buy you that?" She indicated Suzanne's flowery maternity dress.

She hadn't, but Suzanne wondered if Greta knew that her parents had paid for her IVF treatments.

Greta drifted away. People kept coming up to Suzanne with good wishes. After a while she went to the edge of the roof to enjoy the view of the Hudson and the George Washington Bridge. As she watched the boats she wondered if Martha's son had moved the boxes out of her mother's room.

There was a commotion and it turned out that someone had knocked over a bowl of guacamole. Suzanne wished she could help Eddie clean up the mess. As she'd crouch beside him—the skin on his sweet scalp would look soft and new—Marc would see them and, worried her position was somehow endangering the baby, he'd shout at her, "What in the hell are you doing?"

"Hey man," Eddie would tell him quietly, "watch your language!"

Suzanne felt something she was sure was a contraction.

When she rushed to tell Marc, he was surprisingly calm.

"Don't tell your parents. Just tell them we're tired. Say you're tired." She worried that if they knew, there'd be champagne and flowers waiting in her hospital room. She wanted it to be just her and Marc and their baby.

The obstetrician on call said it was too early and sent them home. Marc kept telling her to rate her contractions on a scale of one to ten; he'd ask if she wanted any of the various things their birthing instructor had suggested. "Are you sure you don't want to call your mom?"

"You can do one thing for me."

He was jiggling his foot.

"Turn off the radio."

Fully dressed except for their shoes, they lay on top of their bed.

"Do you think Greta knows that your parents paid for my IVF?"

"No idea."

Her contractions seemed to be diminishing. "I thought that was so nice, Eddie's shaving his head for Carmen." She waited for him to say something. "Would you do that? For me? Shave your head?"

He didn't say anything.

When she'd asked, she hadn't thought much about it, but now she was uneasy. "If I had chemo and lost my hair, would you shave your head?"

"Why are we talking about this? You're jinxing yourself. And you're jinxing the baby!"

"Don't give me that."

He didn't say anything.

"Would you?"

"I don't know."

"You don't know?" She felt like a lawyer.

"I'm not sure."

"Because of your clients? You wouldn't show your support for your wife because of the greedy little shits you work for?" That was it! She never should have married him. "I'm out of here!" she'd tell him. She'd said it to other men. She could live with her single friend who'd gotten pregnant from a sperm bank. She and Marc could share custody. (Of course he—and his family—would be vicious.) Her contractions were definitely weakening. What if the baby never came out? She told herself that was just the kind of stupid thing Marc would think.

"It's not my clients," he said softly.

"You're mumbling."

"The problem isn't my clients, my clients can deal."

"Well?"

"Don't be mad, but I'd be worried about my bald spot."

"Your bald spot? You don't have a bald spot, I told you, what is the matter with you? And what does your bald spot have to do with it?" She sat up so she could see him better.

He was biting a cuticle. "What if I shaved my head, in some sort of solidarity with you, and then it never grew back in that spot? Like a kind of reverse stimulation."

"What are you talking about?" Exhausted, she lay back against the pillows.

"Your hair would grow back, you have a lot of hair. But I'd have a bald spot for the rest of my life! Anyway, can we stop talking about this?"

She was about to ask, "Would you shave it for the baby?" But she knew—even if he didn't know it yet—that he'd do it. She made herself take deep breaths, and after a while she calmed down. "I don't know whether to laugh or cry." It was getting dark. The next time she'd be in bed at twilight, their baby would be with her.

She'd imagined that when her water broke she'd be in the lobby chatting with Eddie about something like the weather. When it actually happened, though, much later that night, as her contractions intensified and she and Marc raced though the lobby, hand in hand, Eddie was so far from her thoughts that it was as if he'd never even existed.

Half-Kidding

"Could you do me a favor and watch him for a second? I left his bottle in the car." Gesturing toward the baby sleeping in the stroller, he ran out of the café before Jessica, who wasn't even his waitress, could stop him.

Over the past few weeks she'd been vaguely aware of him. He'd bring in his baby and do something on his computer for an hour or two; occasionally he'd talk intensely on his phone. Jessica had a feeling he was a businessman. Mid-thirties, with dark curly hair, he had a deliberate-looking dark stubble and wore expensive-looking jeans and plaid shirts unbuttoned enough to show his hairy chest. It was February, and Jessica had been working at Ray's Coffee since August when, at the last minute, she'd decided to take a year off before starting grad school.

At first she'd enjoyed things like learning how to make satiny foam for cappuccino and chatting with the customers. They'd say, "Thank you *so* much" when she'd bring them water, and most left generous tips. But other customers were annoying. They'd earnestly tell her how they "needed" to be near a window, or they'd keep asking if she was sure their coffee was decaf. What she'd think of as packs of moms would let their shrill children make a mess. Occasionally a writer/professor type would recommend a book or movie they assumed she'd never heard of. One or two customers had asked her to keep an eye on their computer while they went to the bathroom, but no one had left her with a baby.

He was only gone a few minutes. "Sorry. Thanks." He held out his hand. "Aron."

She ignored his hand. "First of all, I'm not even your waitress. And even if I were, you can't just do that…"

"I did it!" He smirked. "Just kidding. Sorry." He pointed to the now-awake baby. "This is Max. Max, smile at the pretty lady."

Jessica didn't look at the child. "Don't ever do that again." She walked away.

She'd never been rude to a customer, but it had been a difficult day. Several customers had moved to window seats, leaving her to clean up the tables they'd abandoned. One woman's stingy tip included a lot of pennies. A man whose toddler had dropped food all over the floor made no effort to clean it up. And always, as if she had a chronic, low-grade headache, Jessica felt uneasy about her life. She was almost twenty-seven and regretted postponing grad school. Instead of waitressing, she should have let her mother, who worked for an arts foundation, use her connections to get her some kind of internship. It had been almost a year since she'd had a boyfriend, and she wasn't dating much. Her closest friend had moved to California. At least Ray, the owner, wasn't around to witness this whole episode with Aron, who was right at her heels.

"I said I was sorry."

He wore a wedding ring. She could hear him apologizing, over and over, to his poor wife.

"Forget it," she said. "I shouldn't have lost my temper. It's fine. Really."

"Promise?"

She could tell he was used to taking advantage of people and getting away with it.

Natalia, the other waitress, around her age, was fill-ing sugar bowls slowly as she watched them. She worked more hours and was usually there during Jessica's shift. Romanian, she was self-conscious about her English, which sounded pretty good to Jessica. Both women had their hair pulled back in a ponytail and wore ruffled black aprons that said "Ray's." Natalia was taller and broader than Jessica and, with sallow, slightly pockmarked skin, not as attractive. The women were polite to each other, but hadn't become friends.

"You look cute when you're mad," Aron said. "Just kidding. Half-kidding."

She wondered if he was unfaithful. Occasionally a cus-tomer, usually an older man, would flirt with her, but so far there hadn't been any problems. The next time Aron sat at her table she'd "forget" to bring him water and, if he asked for decaf, she'd make it a point to give him regular. In less than six months she'd be out of New York, studying to be a teacher and on the other side of the espresso machine. For once she was disappointed she had no customers. She had a feeling that if she tried to escape to the kitchen Aron would follow her, so she went into the bathroom.

Seeing herself in the mirror, Jessica thought about how much better she looked when she wasn't at work and her shoulder-length dark hair could be loose. She moved the wastebasket closer to the door—her own idea: one of the things she disliked about her job was that custom-ers, especially women, would wash and dry their hands and then, trying to avoid germs, they'd use a paper towel to open the door; but then, not knowing what else to do with the towel, they'd leave it on their table for the wait-ress to deal with.

When she came out she had several new customers, including Mary. Short and heavy, with very short, very black hair, she wore baggy clothes and was mildly retarded. Jessica found it hard to tell how old she was, but assumed that she was in her forties. Although she dreaded waiting on her, she was always touched by the pleasure Mary took in the too-cold pastries and in drinking tea from the dingy white mugs.

"I'm coming here for chocolate cake for my birthday," Mary announced loudly. She often talked about her birthday.

Jessica smiled, but didn't ask when it was.

She got so busy she didn't notice Aron leaving. Although she'd meant to ask Natalia what kind of tip he'd left, there was another rush and she forgot.

On her day off Jessica was on her way to her neighborhood diner for breakfast when she saw Aron, in an expensive-looking leather jacket—there was an air about him as if he knew he was attractive—pushing Max in his stroller.

"So where are you going?" he asked.

"Um, what makes you think I'd tell you?" She reminded herself he was a customer. "Sorry, I haven't had my coffee yet."

They established that she wasn't going to work.

"Good. Because I'm buying you coffee—to thank you for 'babysitting'—and the coffee at your place tastes like shit."

"That's nice of you, but you don't have to thank me." They were approaching the diner. "See you at Ray's." Wiggling her fingers at Max, she said, "Bye-bye."

Aron followed her in. She didn't hold the door open for his big stroller and was tempted to walk out, but she worried he'd make a scene. Although the Dominican waitresses didn't joke with her the way they did with other customers, they'd begun to bring her café con leche right away without her asking.

She chose a booth in the back. Many of the customers were eating dinner and looked like they'd worked all night.

Aron slid in across from her, leaving Max's stroller partially blocking the aisle.

Max whimpered. Aron jiggled his stroller. Jessica was disappointed when he quieted down—she'd hoped they'd leave.

Aron opened his menu. "You're a cheap date."

She wouldn't give him the satisfaction of responding.

As the waitress took their order, Jessica decided that if he didn't leave a decent tip, she'd secretly add to it. Actually, she'd leave something regardless. And why should she do it secretly?

"You look pretty with your hair down."

She felt in her purse for a barrette so she could pull her hair back in a ponytail, but there was nothing. "By the way, I have a boyfriend."

"That's okay."

"Excuse me?"

"I don't mind if you have a boyfriend." He smirked.

It annoyed her that she and Aron were both wearing jeans and black tops—hers a tee shirt that was getting small on her, his a shirt with several open buttons.

"Can I ask you something?" he said.

She just looked at him.

Max was whimpering.

"Do a lot of customers hit on you?"

"No."

He took Max out of his stroller and gave him a bottle. Max drank quickly, staring at his father with his big dark eyes. His cheeks looked smooth and soft. Jessica wished his little shirt didn't say, "Birth: Nailed it!"

Taking a sip of his café con leche, Aron said, "This is twice as good and probably costs half as much as you know where."

Max burped loudly. If Aron weren't so irritating, it would have been funny. Jessica wished her toast would come so she could eat it quickly and leave.

"Can I ask you something else?"

"Would it stop you if I said no?" She thought she sounded like some tough-talking waitress type.

"Are you Jewish?"

"Excuse me?"

He put Max back in his stroller. "You're Jewish, right?"

"My mom is. But we've never been religious." She told herself to just say yes or no.

"To Hitler you'd be a Jew."

"Excuse me?"

"Just kidding. Half-kidding."

Jessica slowly shook her head as if in amazement at what a jerk he was. But the strong coffee was making her more cheerful, and she was vaguely curious about him.

"So you're a stay-at-home dad?"

"I used to work for a hedge fund, but for now I'm just consulting. In September, I'm back in an office." He spoke to Max. "No more stay-at-home dad."

Her life would change then, too. When she was feeling

optimistic, she'd think of this strange time as her gap year.

"Do you ever think of being a stay-at-home dad as a kind of gap year?" she asked him. "I mean, sometimes I think of waitressing that way."

"Does it have something to do with the Gap store?"

She laughed. "It's like a time between your real lives. Most people do it right before or after college."

"That's the stupidest thing I ever heard."

When the waitress brought Jessica's toast, Aron ordered more coffee. Jessica usually had just one cup, but she ordered another. She needed it.

"Of course I also manage my own investments."

Of course he wanted her to know he had money.

"Your wife works?" She'd keep mentioning his wife.

He said Carolyn was a CEO at a "major" women's clothing chain.

"Can I ask you something else?" He smiled.

"Ask me something else."

Max was looking at her solemnly.

"What are you going to do for a job when Ray's goes out of business because their coffee is shit?"

"I'm going to be a teacher, I'm not sure yet which grade." Saying it made her feel the usual uneasiness. She suffered from test anxiety. No matter how well prepared she was, she'd freeze. It had taken her a long time to finish college and then prepare for and take the GRE exam. Her other problem with teaching was she'd never had any particular desire to do it. But she didn't know what else to do.

"Teaching, that's your dream?" Aron asked her.

There was something almost child-like about 'dream," especially coming from him. She was also surprised that he sensed her ambivalence.

"Actually, in college I took a workshop in cabaret singing." It had been a while since she'd talked about it. "I could always carry a tune, but I never starred in high school musicals or anything like that." She could feel the caffeine making her chatty. "Our 'final' was to perform at a 'nightclub'—the gym—mainly for friends and family." Wearing a black cocktail dress and her dead grandmother's diamond earrings, she sang "Autumn Leaves," even though it was spring, She'd been less nervous and enjoyed it more than she'd thought. She'd also ended up dating a classmate's brother who'd been in the audience. "I would have loved to do it for the rest of my life, but back in the city I couldn't even get an audition." She pushed away her mostly uneaten toast. "Anyway, I've got to go."

"You're wasting good food?"

Max was getting restless, and finally Aron gestured for their waitress. Jessica decided to let him pay.

"Thank you for breakfast," she said primly.

"As I said, you're a cheap date."

She couldn't wait to get out of there.

After the overheated restaurant, the cold air felt good.

"Thanks again." She walked away quickly.

He was right next to her. "If you live in the neighborhood, I'll walk you home."

She was vague about where her apartment was.

They hadn't even gone a block when Aron stopped in front of a drycleaners.

"Wait just a minute. I'll be right back."

As he struggled to get Max's stroller through the door, she walked away.

A few minutes later he caught up with her. "Now how long did that take?"

"I don't like doing my own errands. I'm not about to tag along for yours."

Among the pile of clothes folded over the handle of the stroller, she could see what looked like a bright blue dress.

"Actually, I'm not going home," she lied. "I'm meeting a friend." She wished she'd said she was meeting her boyfriend.

Aron shrugged and let her go.

Back in her apartment, a studio she'd inherited from her grandmother, she felt at loose ends. She'd been in school for so long, or working with some test-taking expert or psychotherapist or just studying on her own, that she felt uneasy about her unstructured time. As she often did, she stood in front of a painting of a black hydrangea against a green background that hung above her non-working fireplace. Her grandmother had painted it in an art class for seniors, and it was Jessica's favorite thing in the apartment.

"Hydrangeas aren't black," Aron would say. Then he'd calculate what the apartment was worth.

"I wish she were alive and living here instead of me," Jessica would tell him—not that he'd care.

She tried to read, but couldn't concentrate. After a while she decided to do something she hadn't done in several years. She stood in front of her mirror and started singing "My Funny Valentine." She'd wanted to sing it at her cabaret concert, but their teacher had chosen Colette, the star of the class. Jessica had heard that Colette was an understudy in an off-Broadway musical. Although many of Jessica's former classmates were ahead of her in their careers, Colette was the only one she dreaded having to wait on at Ray's.

"But don't change a hair for me/Not if you care for me," she sang to her reflection and then, abruptly, she stopped singing.

The next few days at work were especially dreary. Mary talked repeatedly and loudly about her birthday. Several customers moved to window seats. An elderly man kept making corny jokes, and when he suddenly was silent, Jessica worried she'd been glaring at him. When she got off work at five it was drizzling, she'd forgotten her umbrella, and Aron—without Max but with a large, shaggy, caramel-colored dog—seemed to come out of nowhere. He put his umbrella over her head. She hoped Natalia wasn't looking out the window.

A bicyclist riding on the sidewalk sped past them.

"Get off the sidewalk," Aron yelled after him. He smiled at Jessica. "I want you to sing me a song."

"You better not have been waiting for me."

"I'll walk you home."

"Are you kidding?" She didn't wait for him to answer. "You're never coming to my apartment." She moved out from under his umbrella. "And I'm never going to sing for you."

He put the umbrella back over her head. "I'm not going to lie and say I have a friend in the music business who might help you...."

"What the fuck is it with you?"

"You shouldn't curse. It doesn't become you."

"It doesn't become me? You sound like my grandmother."

"I just want you to sing me a song."

"As I told you, I'm not a singer. I don't sing any more. I've got to go. Don't wait for me again."

She walked quickly in the opposite direction from her apartment. When she realized he wasn't following her, she slowed down. It occurred to her that his appearing out of the rainy night to ask her to sing him a song was like something from a fairy tale.

Max's new nanny worked longer hours than his old one, and Aron spent more time at the café. He'd do annoying things like ostentatiously bring in a coffee container from Starbucks and then, with a flourish, show Jessica that it was empty. Once he interrupted her while she was taking someone's order to ask if she'd keep an eye on his computer—"and my camera, and don't forget my bag from Saks"—while he went to the bathroom.

She gave him an incredulous look, then realized that he was kidding or, as he'd say, half-kidding. (The other customer was amused.)

She noticed that although he didn't hesitate to talk to her when she was busy, when he was on his computer he'd often ignore her, even if she was bringing his coffee or refilling his water glass. Sometimes he'd be on the phone and leave without even waving goodbye.

When he wasn't ignoring her, he wouldn't let her alone. "You look a little pale without lipstick," he'd tell her when it had worn off or she wasn't wearing any. "Pretty girl!" he'd say when she wore it.

She asked herself if he could be gay, but decided he was just a kind of jerk she hadn't encountered before. If he weren't a customer, she would have told him off.

But when he'd bring Max in, dressed in one of his little shirts that said things like, "Keep calm and eat bacon!" she'd laugh in spite of herself.

Sometimes he'd say that if she wouldn't sing to him, he'd sing to her. Off-key, he'd launch into "99 Bottles of Beer." Or he'd hum the theme from *Titanic*, which she'd told him she hated. She'd say he was embarrassing her, but in a way she liked being reminded of that time in her life.

One day after Aron noted that she wasn't wearing lipstick, she explained—with mock patience—how lipstick tends to wear off. He didn't really respond, but the next time she saw him he said he'd discussed "your lipstick problem" with Carolyn. "She says you should outline your lips with a special pencil first. You can get them in Sephora."

"You discussed my lipstick? With your wife?"

He shrugged.

She was curious about Carolyn, and although Aron wasn't expansive, he didn't seem to mind talking about her.

Carolyn wore bright red lipstick. She and Aron had grown up on Long Island, but they'd met in Manhattan. Both of her parents were lawyers. She made fun of self-help books, but she liked to read them. She'd named their dog Leeza.

"Leeza? That's unusual," said Jessica. "Is it a female?"

"First she wanted to call her Lola. Then she made up 'Leeza' because you have to smile when you say 'Leeza.'" He smiled.

"She sounds nice. Too bad she's married to you."

He mentioned that Carolyn had been in Ray's a few days before.

"You were here with Carolyn?"

"She was with one of her colleagues."

"You didn't tell her to introduce herself to me?"

"I don't think you were around. Maybe it was your day off."

Jessica was surprised to feel disappointed.

"What does she look like?"

"She's about your height and has blonde hair—that wasn't always blonde." He smirked.

Jessica began to study every thirty-or forty-something blonde woman who came in.

She suspected he had affairs, but although he was flirty, he never tried to touch her. And although she knew he was attractive, he was so impossible that she wouldn't have been interested in him even if he were single. Her tough waitress persona—which he apparently found amusing—felt almost anti-sexual.

They didn't talk personally. When she asked if being a stay-at-home dad was hard for him, he just said, "I enjoy making money. I don't care where I do it."

When he asked what she'd done the night before, she'd say, "What makes you think I'd tell you?"

He'd laugh.

She kept forgetting to bring up her boyfriend.

More and more often, when she was through working he'd be waiting for her outside, with Max and/or Leeza. "So when are you going to sing me a song?"

"Never. I'm never going to sing you a song."

"Okay, okay."

"Or walk your dog."

"Okay!"

"Or babysit."

"Did I ask you to babysit?"

Her friend Sophie wanted to fix her up with a lawyer, and although he didn't sound promising, Jessica agreed to go to a magic show with him.

As soon as the magician started recruiting people to assist him with rope tricks, Jessica worried that he'd choose her: she knew that whatever he asked her to do, she'd freeze as if she were taking a test. She also knew that even though the magician was on the other side of the room, there was something about her anxiety that would attract his attention.

When he came over and asked her to volunteer, she said No in such a way that instead of joking the way he had with everyone else who'd refused, he just quickly went on to someone else.

After the show she and the lawyer talked about getting together again. She had a feeling that neither of them would pursue it.

The next time she saw Aron and he began teasing her about her gap year, on an impulse she said, "I'm not even sure I want to go to grad school."

"So don't go."

"That's the stupidest thing I ever heard."

But then she wondered if maybe he was right. Maybe she could do something in the music business. Or her mother could help her get an internship at a non-profit. As her therapist used to say, she had choices. For the rest of her shift, she was euphoric.

But before long she decided to at least try grad school.

Aron began to ask her for favors, like following Max's

nanny when she took him to the park.

"It'll be a nice walk for you. Just see if she pays any attention to him. Stay for maybe fifteen minutes—not even that."

"I'm not going to spy on your nanny."

He showed her the woman's picture.

"She looks nice. I feel sorry for her, working for you." She felt like a grouch from a sitcom.

He laughed.

Once he called the café—Natalia answered—and asked Jessica if she'd walk Leeza after work. "Just this once. I'll pay you."

"I'm never going to walk your dog. Ever."

"Okay, okay. Don't have a cow."

"Don't have a cow? Who even talks that way?" She imagined him smirking.

When she got off the phone she thought about telling Natalia how annoying he was, but she was afraid it would sound like they were having an affair.

Although her schedule was erratic, he seemed to know when she was working.

When he hadn't come she'd catch herself checking her lipstick; and although she didn't want to admit it, when she'd come out of the bathroom or kitchen and he'd be there—her job felt less dreary.

Jessica mentioned to her friend Sophie that one of Max's shirts said, "I love boobies!" Her point was how vulgar it was, but Sophie was confused. "Who's Max?"

"I never told you about Aron?"

"Aron?"

Jessica felt uncomfortable explaining how he'd asked,

"Is teaching your dream?" and waited in the rain to tell her, "I want you to sing me a song."

"Believe me, if he weren't a customer I wouldn't go near him."

"Just be careful!" Sophie said.

"Listen, as soon as school starts I'll never see him again." Jessica hoped she didn't sound defensive.

"You sound a little defensive."

When Jessica left work one spring-like afternoon, Aron was parked outside in a black SUV, with Max and Leeza in the back.

"Hey pretty lady, wanna get an ice cream?" He opened the door. "Max really wants you to come."

"It's tacky to use Max like that." But she got in.

She rarely rode in SUV's and she liked being high up. When she was growing up her parents only drove to and from their country house. It always surprised her now when her friends with cars drove all around the city.

Almost right away, Max started crying.

"He must have dropped his pacifier," said Aron. "Can you look for it?"

As Jessica took off her seatbelt, she imagined a crash: her family would find out that not only had she died because she wasn't wearing a seatbelt, but she'd been with a married man.

Later he slammed on his brakes.

"My God!" she cried out. "You almost hit that cyclist."

"First of all I was nowhere near him. And second, he didn't signal."

"Please don't drive like a maniac."

He shrugged.

As it got warmer they drove to the Botanical Gardens, the Cloisters, the Brooklyn Museum—places she hadn't been to since middle school.

One day he wouldn't tell her where he was going, and she was intrigued. There was a lot of traffic, and when he pulled into the parking lot of the Brooklyn Ikea, Jessica was furious. "You're kidding."

But of course he wasn't.

"I just want to see if they have a certain lamp. It won't take long. I promise."

"Your promises are shit."

"I bet you've never even been here."

"That's exactly right. And I'll never go in."

"Good. You can try their Swedish meatballs and lingonberry juice."

"Fuck you."

"Come on. Expand your world a little."

"'Expand your world a little,'" she mimicked. She looked out the window. The SUV was parked at an angle and took up half of the next space. "You don't even know how to park."

"I'm protecting my $70,000 investment."

"I'm protecting my $70,000 investment," she mimicked. She refused to go inside and wouldn't even wave goodbye to Max.

She was looking up how to get back to her apartment by public transportation when they came back.

"They didn't have what I wanted."

"Good." She couldn't face trying to get home by public transportation.

"Anyway, I got us dinner." He took several containers

out of a shopping bag.

"I'm not hungry."

They ate Swedish meatballs and drank lingonberry juice. When Aron gave Max a taste of the juice, he made a face as if he hated it, then screamed for more. Jessica laughed and laughed. She thought everything was delicious and was tempted to steal one of Aron's meatballs. After they'd cleaned up and were ready to go, Aron said, "Wait a minute!"

"What now?"

He took out his handkerchief and gently wiped away her lingonberry mustache.

"You better not have blown your nose in that," she murmured.

"Oops!" he said. "I'm afraid I might have." Then he said, "Just kidding."

On the drive back Max fell asleep. Jessica closed her eyes, and when she woke up it took her a minute to remember where she was.

"Were you dreaming about me?"

"I wasn't sleeping."

There was heavy traffic, and the driver beside them kept honking. Aron opened his window. "Nice horn!" he yelled. "What else did you get for Christmas?"

"You're yelling," Jessica said.

"So? He's an asshole." He closed his window. "Don't have a cow."

"You're so different from everyone I know," she said.

He looked pleased.

She was pleased, then uneasy. On some dull day when she was bored or lonely, she didn't want to find herself having sex with Aron. She couldn't avoid seeing him at work, but she could still pull back. Although he'd started to walk her home, she'd find excuses to get out of it. And she'd never again get into his stupid $70,000 SUV.

On Mary's birthday—despite the warm spring day, she wore overalls—Jessica cut her an enormous piece of chocolate cake, found and lit a candle, and asked Natalia if she'd join her in singing Happy Birthday.

"I wouldn't feel comfortable," said Natalia.

Jessica shrugged. She looked forward to never seeing her again.

There were several other customers, and as Jessica approached Mary's table she was self-conscious. But she sang, "Happy Birthday," and when Mary blew out her candle all the customers clapped. In a way Jessica wished that Aron had been there. She was also glad he wasn't.

She worked the next evening. It was raining and had rained all day, and business was slow. She heard Natalia tell their only customer that it had been quiet all afternoon. Ray called and said that if no one else came in during the next hour, she and Natalia could close early.

They immediately put up the Closed sign and locked the door. After they'd cleaned up, put away their aprons, and turned off most of the lights, Natalia asked her to stay a little longer. "There's something I want to say to you."

Jessica had a feeling Natalia would ask if she and Aron were having an affair, and she looked forward to telling her they weren't.

They made tea and brought their dingy white mugs to a table by the window. For a few minutes they looked out at the rainy street. Natalia took out her ponytail. In the dim light, her acne scars didn't show. She had pretty brown eyes.

"I feel bad I didn't sing 'Happy Birthday' to Mary."

Relieved that was what she wanted to say, Jessica smiled. "Don't worry about it."

"My whole life I've been shy. And then it's harder here, because of my English."

"Your English is fine. It's good."

A customer was outside and gestured he wanted to come in. They shook their heads and he went away. With the steady rain, darkening sky and just the two of them by the window, the café was almost cozy. Jessica wondered if, at this late date, she and Natalia could become friends.

Natalia talked about growing up on a farm in Romania. Her boyfriend was a computer technician. They lived in Jackson Heights.

When Jessica told her about going to grad school, Natalia kept saying how lucky she was.

Jessica mentioned her test anxiety. "I'm sort of dreading the whole thing."

"I don't feel sorry for you," Natalia said almost angrily. "It's just a few years, and then you'll have a good job for the rest of your life."

Jessica wasn't sure what to say. Another customer wanted to come in. They decided to go.

A few days later Aron was waiting outside in the SUV. "Max wants you to come with us to Battery Park City."

"I'm going out with my boyfriend."

He shrugged.

Jessica was on her way to work—it was her last week —when Aron called. Max's nanny was home sick and although Max was fine, Aron was queasy. Carolyn was in Boston trying to get an earlier flight home.

"I need you," Aron said.

She wasn't sure she believed him. "I'm on my way to work."

"Please."

She called and told Natalia she couldn't come in. She didn't say why, and Natalia didn't ask.

Jessica was amused that Aron's modern high-rise was called Stonehenge.

"Thank God!" Aron said when he opened the door. In gym shorts and a tee shirt, he looked pale. After giving her Max's bottle and showing her where Leeza's leash was, he ran back to bed.

Max didn't object to her holding him. As she sat on the sofa and gave him his bottle, she hoped it wasn't Carolyn's breast milk. When Aron had fed him, she'd never really thought about it.

The living room was big, with a lot of dark furniture. On the mantle there was a photograph of Aron, Max, and a pretty woman with red lips and blonde hair. Although she wore a skirt and blazer, she was barefoot—as if she'd just finished work and had kicked off her high heels. Max drank quickly, staring into Jessica's eyes.

"Hi Max," she said softly. His cheek looked so smooth and soft, she kissed it. After he finished his bottle they played peek-a-boo. When he started whimpering, she realized he was wet.

She found his diapers and managed to change him, but even with a clean diaper and dry clothes—she couldn't find any of his funny shirts—he wouldn't stop crying. She tried to distract him with several of his toys, but nothing helped. She worried that if he didn't calm down, Aron would get out of his sickbed to help. Finally, not knowing what else to do, she held Max close and sang, "Mairzy Doats," a nonsense song her mother used to sing to her. Jessica remembered singing it to a boyfriend once when she was drunk. When she was through they'd had sex.

"A kiddley divey too/Wouldn't you?" she sang softly, her lips almost touching Max's dark curls. Suddenly she looked around, as if Aron had tiptoed in and had been listening the whole time.

No one was there.

After Max finally quieted down, Leeza barked as if she wanted to go out. "I know, I know," Jessica told her. "But I have to give Aron some water first." She shifted Max to her other hip. "You know what, Max? You're getting to be a really big boy!" She felt as if she were in a play.

The kitchen sink was full of dirty dishes. There were pink rubber gloves near the dish drainer. Jessica picked one up, then quickly put it down. She found a clean glass, filled it with water, and knocked on what she assumed was Aron's bedroom door.

Ashen and sweaty-looking, he lay on top of messy sheets

"I brought you some water."

He groaned.

"You have to drink something or you'll get dehydrated." Her mother used to tell her that. "Lift your head a little."

"Okay, okay." He didn't move.

Max was squirming in her arms. She brought the glass closer to Aron's lips. "Just a few sips."

Her mother used to say that, too. Jessica had probably

said it to a boyfriend who'd had pneumonia. She couldn't remember any boyfriend ever taking care of her when she was sick. In a way, it was something to look forward to.

Aron took a small sip, then lay back down and closed his eyes.

Jessica shifted Max to her other hip and tiptoed out, Leeza at her heels.

As she lowered Max into his stroller, he waved his arms with excitement.

Leeza barked.

"Okay, okay, I hear you. Are you guys ready to go to the park?" Maybe Carolyn had been able to get on an earlier plane and they'd meet in the lobby. Seeing Jessica with Max and Leeza, she'd seem confused.

"I'm from Ray's Café," Jessica would say. "The waitress?"

"The waitress. Of course." She'd move closer to the stroller. "Thank you *so* much." Her lips would be very red.

Leeza began butting her head against Jessica's legs and Max was squirming, but Jessica wasn't sure how to work the safety harness on his stroller. For a minute she froze and her mind went blank as if it were a test. But then she got started. And although the last strap looked as if it would be tricky to fasten, she knew it was something she could do.

Do You Know What
I'm Not Telling You?

It was supposed to be a romantic weekend in Manhattan, but Sam, their toddler, had been sick and Jill and Carl didn't get away until Saturday afternoon. As soon as they closed their hotel room door Carl gestured toward the bed, piled with many large and small pillows, and said, "I could use a nap."

Jill would have preferred going for a walk, but she took off her clingy sweater and tight skirt and got under the spread with him. His rule for naps was that you should keep them short and never get under the sheets. They wouldn't have sex until later because he preferred to do it before they went to sleep for the night. In their late thirties, they'd been married six years.

When she woke up the room was dark and Carl was in the bathroom. She went to the window. It was a grey mid-November day, brightened by many yellow cabs. She called to check on Sam. The sitter said he was fine and gave him the phone. He didn't say anything, but hearing him breathe into the receiver, Jill could see his fat cheeks and soft pink mouth. "I love you," she said. Carl flushed the toilet.

"We should call Sam," he said as he came out.

"I called. He's fine."

"Good. Let's not talk about Sam." When they were on a "date," they'd try not to talk about Sam.

Jill took a shower, even though the bathroom still smelled.

When she came out, wrapped in a skimpy towel, Carl was sitting on the bed dressed in his usual khaki pants and plaid shirt. Since they'd been together his brown hair was a little longer, and his glasses were more stylish. Still, he looked like the college professor he was.

He reached for her hand and pulled her down next to him. "Let's talk about having another child."

They'd discussed it before. He thought he wanted one; she wasn't sure. She'd say, truthfully, that part of her wanted to go back to work. She didn't say she wasn't sure she wanted another child with him. He was a loving dad, but there always seemed to be a problem. When he was awakened at night—and Sam woke up a lot— Carl had trouble falling back asleep. He worried about Sam's every sniffle and got queasy when Sam threw up or had diarrhea. When Sam had a playdate or was playing by himself or just staring into space, Carl would hover.

Jill made up her mind. She twisted one of her auburn corkscrew curls around her finger, something she did when she was nervous. "Sorry, but I'm ready to go back to work." She adjusted her towel.

"Okay," he said slowly.

"But are you going to be okay with just our Sammy?" she asked him.

He hesitated. "I think I am." He took off his glasses and put them on again. "Listen, I never imagined I'd have such a wonderful son. Or…." He put his hand on the still-damp skin above her breasts. "Or that I'd be lucky enough to get a juicy plum like you."

Most of her boyfriends had been writers or musicians, and after a while she'd feel as if she were always sitting around watching them write or compose or practice their instrument. She felt like a failure in other ways. After college she couldn't get a job in publishing or any kind of arts organization and reluctantly accepted a position as an office manager for a large law firm. Although it turned out she loved being part of the busy office, and looked forward to all the birthday and holiday celebrations with her co-workers, almost everyone she knew made more money doing something more prestigious. And always in the background, even after years of psychotherapy, she mourned her mother, who'd died when Jill was twenty.

At first she'd had her doubts about Carl. He tended to hover. When she'd be about to go somewhere by herself, he'd keep offering to "walk" her, and when they weren't together, he'd call a lot. Still, his eagerness to keep her company, even when she was doing boring chores, reminded her of her favorite fairy tale: after Beauty told the Beast that she couldn't reciprocate his love, he'd continue to sit with her every night as she ate her dinner—and she'd enjoy his company. Carl was her first boyfriend who wouldn't let her call herself a fuck-up. And with all his rules and anxieties, he made her feel free-spirited, almost like an artist.

She adjusted her towel. "Are you sure you're okay with the idea of never having a daughter?" Although she felt a little sad, she was pretty sure she'd be okay, especially when she was working again.

He joked about the money she was going to make. Then he looked serious. "I want you to be happy."

"Are you going to be unhappy?" She didn't know what she'd do if he said yes.

He didn't hesitate. "No."

She stood up to get dressed. Putting on her bra she remembered, as she sometimes did, the night when Carl, caressing her breasts, suddenly lost his erection.

"Is something wrong?" Despite his fussiness about where and when to have sex, he rarely had trouble staying hard.

"I think I felt a lump," he said softly.

"A lump? Where? In my breast? Which one?"

He couldn't find it again.

She'd been up all night looking for it. The next day her gynecologist couldn't find it either and after sending her for tests which turned out to be normal, he told her to forget about it. For a few weeks she'd worry about the lump every time she and Carl had sex.

As she put on her new high-heeled boots, she was relieved she'd finally made up her mind about having another child and that Carl seemed to accept her decision. But she wished he'd waited and brought it up at home: somehow, their trip no longer seemed particularly romantic.

As soon as they got outside Carl decided that their only "rules" for the trip were not to talk about Sam, not to feel obligated to do anything cultural, and not to end up on the Upper West Side—where she'd grown up and which made her miss her mother. "And we'll have dinner somewhere romantic."

As they walked to Central Park Jill kept expecting to see someone she knew, the way she used to. The gentrified city made her think of how her mother used to look all over Manhattan for "exotic" food like pomegranates and cilantro; she would have loved all the fancy food stores and new restaurants. A carriage driver asked if they wanted a ride around the park. Jill hated being taken for a tourist, and she hated that she'd become one. Her new gray coat with black fur around the cuffs no longer seemed so stylish.

"Every time we come to the city," Carl said, "I think about how we live only half an hour from Grand Central Terminal, but we have four bedrooms, a big yard...."

She knew what was coming.

"Yet we're closer to Manhattan than if we lived in, say...."

"Flatbush," she said.

"It's win-win."

She didn't point out—as she sometimes did—that having to follow a suburban train schedule wasn't the same as being able to take the subway.

"You're not wearing a hat?" Carl said. "I keep telling you, your head is like a chimney—you lose heat through the top."

She'd worn earmuffs since she was a girl and had white ones made of what she'd call bunny fur. She liked it that earmuffs didn't crush her curls the way a hat did. Her boyfriends used to tell her she looked cute in them.

Carl was wearing the wool cap she'd bought him before they were married.

At first he'd worried about the pom-pom on top. "It doesn't look silly?"

"It shows that someone loves you."

The only other present he'd had from a lover was a backpack for Chanukah. "I'm going to wear this hat for the rest of my life," he'd said solemnly.

Carl bought a hotdog from a cart, took a few bites,

and then threw the rest away so he wouldn't spoil his appetite for dinner. When he'd first seen Jill do the same thing with various snacks—she gained weight easily—he'd been horrified by the waste. Then he decided it cost the same whether she ate it or not; and although he didn't have a weight problem, he began throwing snacks away, too. He also copied the way she'd pull out some of the bread from her bagel before toasting it. He couldn't get over how he not only preferred the rough surface of the "scooped" bagel, but it was also less fattening. "Win-win!"

Jill sometimes found this annoying, but then she'd wonder if she were being sexist. Suddenly guilty about depriving him of another child, she patted his pom-pom.

They walked a lot, her boots started to feel tight, and they ended up on the Upper West Side.

"Rule number four…" Carl said.

"Is that rules can always be broken."

They began talking about Sam, laughed at themselves and then, as if by unspoken agreement, went into a children's clothing store. 1970's music was playing. When "You're My First, My Last, My Everything" came on, Jill noticed that the staff as well as the customers— everyone, except Carl—knew the song, and were either subtly moving to the beat or, like her, softly singing along. Carl liked to say that his interest in popular music began and ended with the Beatles. Jill remembered playing him "You're My First…" when they were choosing songs for their wedding. He hadn't been crazy about it.

"And not that it matters," he said, "but the guy sounds like he's been in jail."

She'd googled the singer's bio to prove Carl wrong,

but he was right.

As they left the store with what would be Sam's first denim jacket, Jill thought about how by the time he wore it she'd probably be working. She felt a little sad, but also lucky to have had fourteen months to be a stay-at-home mom.

"Do you know that ninety percent of trips people take in the United States—by trips I'm including errands and getting to work—are by car?" Carl was saying. A sociologist, he was particularly interested in transportation. "And don't forget that the most dangerous part of the trip is the drive to the airport."

Although Jill sometimes had trouble relating to the data he found so satisfying, she admired his passion for his work.

They walked by a nail salon and she looked in the window. "It's not crowded. Let's get pedicures together." This is a test, she thought. Say yes, and maybe we'll have another child. She knew he wouldn't do it.

"You know I don't like that kind of thing."

"Would you mind very much if I got one? You can go to Barnes and Noble."

"Now?"

"Didn't we say we wouldn't feel obligated to do anything cultural?"

"But this is our special weekend."

"We'll have a romantic dinner." She gave him a pleading smile. "I haven't had a pedicure since Sam."

He sighed. "Call me when you're through."

She knew he'd call before she had a chance.

As her feet soaked in the warm water, Jill was aware of the young woman next to her, who also had corkscrew curls. Sometimes when she saw a woman her age with hair like hers, they'd end up talking about bizarre things they'd done when they were young to try to straighten it…she closed her eyes…apparently young women now were more accepting of their hair…"You're my first, my last, my everything," kept going through her head…. she couldn't believe that after her nap she was sleepy…. Hearing giggles and high-pitched voices, Jill opened her eyes. A woman around her age was with several little girls wearing fancy tiaras and skirts that looked like tutus.

Carl came in while her nails were still being painted. He sat in the waiting area and read the Times. Every few minutes he'd look up at her and wave. He wouldn't notice that the woman next to her had curls like hers. He also wouldn't think about how the younger woman made Jill look older. He rushed to pay her bill because even though they had the same credit card, to him it was a kind of gallantry.

At the door Jill turned around. The little girls, perched on high seats, were chattering and giggling. They were very appealing. She wouldn't say anything to Carl, but she suddenly felt what she and her mom used to call sad and soupy.

As they walked down Broadway, Jill was surprised to see that a small barbershop that had been there for as long as she could remember was still there. "Maybe you should get your hair cut before Monday." Carl was chairing some kind of meeting.

"Now?"

She looked in the window. "It's not crowded. And it probably won't be here much longer." He liked supporting small stores from the "old" New York.

"You're sure you wouldn't mind?"

"Go!"

For a while Jill just wandered around. She was starting to forget what restaurants and stores had been where, before all the banks and chain stores. A woman her age who looked just like her friend Emily came out of a brownstone. As she got closer, Jill realized that the woman looked like Emily when she was a lot younger. It was almost twilight. Her mother would have loved the way the tree branches in front of a new restaurant were strung with tiny LED lights. Jill loved it too. She was pleased because even though she was in her old neighborhood, she felt okay.

She was on a side street, near the fence of a schoolyard, when a young man came up to her. Her height, his dark hair was pulled back in a ponytail. He didn't look like a tourist, but she assumed he was going to ask for directions.

"I have a gun." He pointed to a bulge in his pocket. "Shut the fuck up and give me your wallet and phone."

Although several people were nearby, no one seemed aware of what was happening. She opened her purse.

"You can have my wallet, but I left my phone at the hotel. I'm a tourist." The lie just popped out.

As she was taking out her wallet, her phone, also in her purse, rang. She waited for him to shoot her, but for some reason he ran away. A young couple crossed in the middle of the street and walked quickly towards her. The robber was already out of sight. The couple walked past her. Her phone was ringing again.

"All done," Carl said cheerfully. "Where are you?"

Her legs were shaking.

"Are you there?" Carl kept saying.

She was about to tell him how she could have been killed—her eyes were filling with tears—but he'd be upset, and it would spoil the rest of the evening. She'd done enough to spoil his day.

They planned to start walking toward each other.

But she couldn't move, and had to prop herself up against a nearby building. She saw the bulge in the robber's pocket. She couldn't believe she'd risked her life because she didn't want to deal with not having her phone. As soon as she saw Carl she'd probably burst into tears and tell him everything. It came to her that if she'd been killed, it would have been his fault. It was crazy to think that way. Nothing was ever exactly his fault. But she didn't want to be married to him any more.

She was still leaning against the building when Carl appeared.

"It's a little short." He took off his hat to show her his haircut. He didn't ask why she hadn't moved.

"It's fine." A few minutes earlier, she would have cared about his haircut.

"Is everything okay?" Awkwardly, he touched her shoulder. "You're awfully pale."

She knew he thought she was missing her mother. "I'm fine." She looked in his eyes. I'm leaving you. For a minute she was euphoric. Then she realized that breaking up Sam's family would be her biggest fuck-up, ever. But she was still going to do it.

"Are you hungry?" Carl asked.

She saw herself sprawled on the sidewalk. Actually, she was hungry.

They looked for a restaurant, but—unusual for them—kept rejecting each other's choices.

Finally she stopped in front of an ordinary-looking restaurant.

"I thought you weren't in the mood for Italian," Carl said.

"I'm really hungry. This will be fine." She didn't know what she'd do if he said no. She felt so crazy that if it weren't so early in her cycle, she'd think she was getting her period.

"I thought we were going someplace romantic," he said.

Pushing ahead of him, she went in.

The decor was nothing special and she had a feeling the food was nothing special, but the room was quiet, the lights were soft, and their waiter brought a breadbasket with their drinks.

"Wait!" Carl said, as she was about to sip her wine. He lifted his glass. "To us."

Uneasy, she clicked her glass against his.

She ate her roll quickly, but Carl scooped out the filling from his. She made a small pile of the scattered lumps of bread around his plate. She couldn't tell if it was just his haircut, but he looked sad. If she asked him if he was sad about not having another child he'd probably deny it. She tried to pull herself together.

"We managed to find a restaurant that's a throwback to the 1970's," she said. "Like your barbershop." She smiled. "Our trip has a theme!" Carl loved "themes." There was a mirror behind him. She thought she looked like a cadaver.

"You're right, this place is a throwback to the old New York," he said happily.

He summarized a paper about minority voting patterns that one of his colleagues, Alan, had asked him to review.

"Has Alan ever mentioned a girlfriend?" Jill asked when he finished.

"Not as far as I know."

"Maybe he's not even gay," she said. "Maybe he doesn't do anything because he just doesn't want to deal with his sexuality."

"Maybe not doing anything is his way of dealing with it."

It wasn't the kind of thing he usually said. Jill wondered if he sensed she was going to hurt him and was trying to assert himself.

She wanted more wine—she usually had two glasses to Carl's one—but their waiter was busy.

Carl told her about a project he was considering for his upcoming sabbatical.

She'd forgotten he was due for a sabbatical. She wasn't sure how she felt about having him around all day. Actually, they'd probably be separated by then. Maybe he wouldn't realize how devastated he'd be. He'd probably remarry. She'd definitely loosened him up. If he ever had a daughter, she'd loosen him up even more. Jill couldn't imagine what her own life would be like.

"By the way, can you guess which city has the poorest congressional district in the country?" Carl asked her.

She saw the sidewalk splattered with her blood.

"Guess," Carl said.

"Guess what?"

"Which city has the poorest congressional district."

"I don't know." She kept catching glimpses of herself in the mirror.

"Detroit?"

"Guess again."

"Newark? I have no idea."

"I'll give you a hint, a very interesting hint."

Shut the fuck up! She looked into his eyes. I have a gun.

"The same city has both the poorest congressional district and more billionaires than any other city in the world."

"Can we stop this? Please?" Just that morning, she and Sam had been eating bananas and Cheerios. He'd enjoyed feeding her some of his—one for him, and then one for her.

"It's New York!"

"Really?" She rubbed her finger around the inside of her wine glass to get the last few drops.

"New York has the South Bronx, the poorest district, and it has Manhattan, which has more billionaires than all the other cities in the country combined. Isn't that amazing?"

He looked so happy, she felt the way Sam's smile sometimes made her feel: as if her heart were breaking.

Carl pulled out the filling from another roll. She added the new bits of bread to her pile. They talked about how they couldn't wait to see Sam in his new denim jacket.

Their waiter came over.

Carl ordered chicken. "No garlic, please."

When he and Jill were first together and he'd told her he hated garlic, she stopped using it in her cooking. She missed it, though, and after a while she began sneaking it in, first a little and then more and more. Whenever her friend Susie, who knew all about it, came for dinner, she'd start giggling about the garlic. Carl never asked what was so funny, but one night after Susie left he surprised Jill by saying he preferred her other friends.

Her salmon was overcooked. "How's your chicken?"

"It's good." He gave her a taste.

"Guess what?" Pointing her fork at his chicken, she said, "It's loaded with garlic."

"It is not."

"Maybe you haven't tasted garlic for so long, you don't even remember what it's like."

He seemed confused.

Her heart was pounding. "Maybe you've been eating it—in restaurants—for years without knowing it. Maybe you actually like it now."

"I hate garlic." He took her hand—she'd been twisting a curl around her finger—and put it on the table. He didn't like her playing with her hair—it was one of the few things about her that annoyed him.

"I could start adding just a little garlic to our food, and we'd see if you could tell." If he agreed, it could be some kind of test. But she wasn't sure what it would mean.

"That's okay."

"Maybe you'd like it." She looked into his eyes as if daring him to guess the truth.

"That's okay."

When they went out again the air felt warmer and a little damp. They finally agreed on a movie, but by the time they got to the theater it was sold out.

"What now?" he said.

What now? "I'm tired. Maybe we should just go back to the hotel." She didn't want to have sex. She'd make some excuse. The streetlights looked hazy, and the city seemed quiet. "We could walk."

"Watch out for the bike!" he said as they crossed a street.

"He was nowhere near us." She saw the bulge of the gun. When she told Carl she wanted a divorce, he wouldn't know what hit him.

For a while they didn't speak.

A woman down the street was trying to get a cab. Jill called out, "Molly!"

They'd been part of a group of women who'd meet once each season to swap clothes they didn't wear. They'd model the outfits, drink wine, eat take-out. When Jill first moved to the suburbs she'd always come in for it, but after Sam she rarely went. When the group found out she and Carl were getting divorced, they'd tell each other they weren't surprised.

As Molly was describing the new boyfriend she was meeting for dinner, Carl hailed an empty cab. He insisted on opening and then shutting the door for her. When the cab pulled away—Jill could still smell Molly's perfume— he said, "See, you did run into someone you know." He looked happy. "See."

They were a few blocks from their hotel when it started raining. Carl reached for her hand, and they ran the rest of the way. By the time they got inside they were soaked and breathing hard. An older couple, also waiting for the elevator, smiled at them.

After they got to their room and took off their clothes, Jill planned to say she felt too full to make love. But when she put on her sheer white nightgown, and Carl opened his arms and said, "My bride!" she decided to fake it. It was the least she could do.

At one point as he lay on top of her she opened her eyes and looked at him, but his eyes were closed. Eventually she got excited and then, to her surprise, she came.

Carl fell asleep, but she was wide-awake. In the bathroom she saw that her period had come early. She'd always had a heavy flow, and the sheets were probably a mess. Despite his squeamishness Carl wasn't bothered by menstrual blood. Early in their affair he'd told her that when he first learned the facts of life, he couldn't understand why it wasn't recycled for transfusions. She'd loved that.

She looked through her purse and suitcase, but she didn't have a Tampax. The front desk probably had a supply, and there had to be a 24-hour drugstore nearby. But then she found a disposable diaper in a pocket of her suitcase and realized that it might get her through the night.

The diaper was too big to fit in her skimpy underpants. Carl's would be better.

They were actually pretty comfortable, with the diaper's bulk taking up the slack. She'd dampened a towel and was kneeling beside the bed scrubbing the bloody sheet on her side, when Carl woke up. "What are you doing?"

"I got my period. I want to clean the sheets. Can you get up and check your side?"

He was half-asleep, and she had to ask him several times.

Finally he got out of bed. "It's fine." He lay back down. "Just cover it with a towel. We'll leave a big tip."

"I'm not leaving a mess like this."

"They have a way of dealing with these things. Believe me, they've seen worse."

"Give me a minute." There was a clock radio on his night table. It wasn't even midnight.

She was working on the last stain when Carl sat up and turned on his lamp.

She knew he'd have trouble going back to sleep. "I'm almost done."

Soon the stains were much lighter. They'd probably come out in the wash.

"I'm done," she said. "I'm just going to rinse out this towel."

There was a full-length mirror on the bathroom door. The rain had made her hair frizzier than usual, and her sheer nightgown clearly showed Carl's bulky briefs. She hated looking at herself, but it was also funny.

When she came back with towels to put over the damp sheets, Carl was still sitting up.

She spread out the towels on her side, then stepped back from the bed. "Carl?"

"What?"

She twisted a curl around her finger. "Look at me."

"Why?"

"I want you to look at me."

"Are those my briefs?"

Explaining the diaper, she wondered if he'd laugh or find her gross.

He turned off the light and moved over to her side of the bed.

"What are you doing?" she asked him.

He lay down on the towels. "Come to bed, my love."

She hadn't meant it to be a test—but he passed.

Don't Ask Don't Tell

On a late October night in Greenwich Village, the rain was like a mist and it was unseasonably warm. When Jonathan saw a café with an outdoor table sheltered by an awning, he sat down to wait for Carole. Forty-two, he was thin and almost six feet, with dark curly hair and dark eyes. He wore a blazer, dress shirt and jeans. He still couldn't believe that if things went according to plan, in six months he'd be adopting Carole's baby.

It had only been a few weeks since his lawyer friend Peter, also gay, told him about Carole. Two months pregnant, she was twenty-eight and single, lived in New Hampshire, and not only wanted to give up her child, but she preferred a gay male couple or even a gay single man. Whenever Jonathan had vaguely thought about becoming a father he'd assumed he'd have a husband, but he was starting to worry that he'd always be alone. Carole had liked his being a college teacher and that he lived in Manhattan. Although she wasn't Jewish, she seemed pleased that he was. (Apparently when she was in high school a gay male Jewish neighbor had been very important to her.) Jonathan wondered if she also didn't want the baby to have another mother.

The one time he and Carole Skyped he'd worried about her seeing how his apartment had only one bedroom, but when he'd shown her the large dining area that could be converted to a bedroom, she said it was fine. He'd also made clear that in addition to his salary he had enough inherited money to raise a child in an expensive city. Now he was paying for Carole to come down for the weekend so they could talk in person. No papers had been signed, and even when they were, at any point and up to seventy-two hours after the birth she'd be able to legally change her mind.

Suddenly she was there. Her shoulder-length reddish-brown hair looked cheaply dyed, her eye-makeup was too dark for her pale skin, and her front tooth was crooked, but she was prettier than she'd looked on Skype. She wore a faded yellow blouse with embroidered daisies around the collar and sleeves, and black pants. There were several rubber bands on her wrist. Jonathan tried not to look at her belly.

They sort-of hugged, barely touching.

After she sat down she kept glancing at the street. Although Halloween was several days away, it was a Friday night and many people walking by wore costumes.

"It's so exciting to be here," Carole said.

"Your hotel's okay?"

"It's really nice."

He hoped she realized how much it had cost.

When the waiter came Carole ordered a Diet Coke. She told Jonathan he should feel free to have a drink.

The idea of not drinking hadn't even occurred to him.

Although he'd referred to his sabbatical in his application letter, he brought up again how although it would be over in the fall, he'd of course hire a nanny. He felt as if he were at a job interview.

It turned out Carole didn't know what a sabbatical was. She was intrigued.

"Even though I plan to work until my due date,"—she

worked at a thrift shop near Dartmouth College—"I feel like this time in my life, especially since I'm not 'keeping' the baby—it will be like a kind of sabbatical for me."

He wasn't sure what to say.

He didn't know much about her. She'd gone to a community college. The baby's dad (who wasn't in the picture) was white. Peter kept telling him he should thank his lucky stars that she didn't want to be part of the child's life.

"Another thing I want to make clear," Jonathan said, "is that I'll send him or her to private school if that's what...they need."

Carole kept looking at the people walking by. There was a group of small children wearing costumes. Their moms were dressed like princesses or prom queens and had expensively streaked brown or honey-colored hair.

"And as I said in my letter," Jonathan added, "I hope to marry one day."

"Can I ask you something?"

"Of course."

"Do you belong to a temple?"

"Not at the moment." Should he add that he could join one?

When his wine came, he felt too shy to toast the baby.

Carole ordered pizza. Jonathan ordered fish, then changed it to a burger.

After the waiter left, there was a long silence. It felt like an awkward date.

"There's something you should know," Carole said.

"Okay," he said slowly.

"I don't want to find out the baby's sex before it's born. I want it to be a surprise."

He nodded in what he hoped was an encouraging way. He hadn't really thought about finding out early.

"If you want to know, you can talk to the nurse in the office. Just don't tell me. OK?"

"I don't care about the gender." He should have used a different word. "I'm just as happy not to know the sex."

"Okay. But if you change your mind, don't tell me."

"I won't change my mind."

After another silence he talked about his job. He didn't go into how his specialty was modern English poetry, or that his sabbatical project was about Philip Larkin's early poems.

"Do you like Stieg Larson?" Carole asked.

"I keep meaning to read him," he lied.

"He's so good. You'll love him."

She was watching a man walking by who had a snake around his neck. His bare chest and arms were covered with tattoos.

"I've seen him around the Village before," Jonathan said. "He always has that snake. It's not just that it's Halloween."

"I love New York!"

She'd better not expect him to keep paying for her to visit.

When their food came, they ate mostly in silence.

There was an almost full moon. With the streetlights shining through the mist and the small groups of people wearing costumes, everything looked romantic. And here he was, alone and part of what was basically a business transaction.

"I'm thinking about going back to school," Carole said. "Maybe something like social work. Maybe nursing."

"If I can help with your applications in any way, I'd be glad to do it," he said. "I've helped quite a few students." He wasn't going to go into how he'd also helped his former cleaning person and his doorman's son.

His burger was huge and he wasn't used to eating so much meat. He ordered more wine.

Carole was eating her last slice of pizza when the waiter started to take away her plate.

"Hey!" Jonathan said to him. "Where's she supposed to put down her pizza?"

Barely apologizing, the waiter put back her plate.

"Only in New York," Jonathan muttered as the waiter walked away. "They charge exorbitant prices and then they can't wait to get rid of you."

She put what was left of her slice on her plate. "Wow! Thanks. I never would have had the nerve to say anything."

He'd joke to Peter that he felt like her knight in shining armor.

It turned out she didn't expect to go to his apartment (which a friend in real estate had just helped him de-clutter as if he were putting it on the market) or to see him on Saturday. She was leaving early Sunday.

Suddenly he was so cheerful he wondered if he were tipsy.

A witch and a ghost, on bicycles, whizzed by.

As he waited for the check, Carole said, "There's something else I have to tell you."

She'd changed her mind! She'd gotten herself a free weekend in New York, and now she was keeping the baby.

"The thing is," Carole said, "you can't be in the delivery room. My best friend, Diane, she's going to be there with me. We've been friends since first grade...."

"That's fine." He'd thought more about taking the baby back to his apartment than about the birth itself. He realized that actually, he was relieved.

After they signed adoption papers Jonathan found it harder to concentrate on his writing about Larkin. He dated more frequently than he had in a while, but no one seemed promising. Peter invited him to dinner with a gay couple, one of whom was the biological father of their seven year-old daughter. They showed Jonathan many cute pictures, and he briefly wished he'd used his own sperm with a surrogate. He downloaded a Stieg Larsson novel, but although he could see the appeal he couldn't finish it. He went to Barnes and Noble and skimmed childcare books. He googled a few stores that sold furniture for children, but was too superstitious to buy anything yet. He scheduled an appointment with the psychotherapist he'd stopped seeing several years before. He was surprised when, as Jonathan told him about the adoption, the therapist got teary.

Once a week he called Carole. He'd ask how she was feeling, and she'd say she was fine. He'd ask about her job, and she'd say they were busy or not very busy. She never asked him anything.

One day she said she'd just been to her obstetrician and had heard the baby's heartbeat.

"Too bad you weren't there."

Was she trying to make him feel bad? Should he offer to come to New Hampshire one weekend? He didn't know her well enough to read her signals.

Their best conversation was when he mentioned he'd seen Conan O'Brien at Starbucks.

Jonathan decided that if this didn't work out, he'd never try to be a father again.

In February Carole invited him to New Hampshire.

"You can meet my obstetrician, Dr. Vo. I really love her. And you can hear the baby's heartbeat."

He rented a car, arrived in the late afternoon, and was amused that the inexpensive hotel Carole had recommended gave him a suite with two sinks and three beds. Relieved when Carole texted she had to work late and couldn't have dinner with him, he went for a walk. There were a few office buildings, a luncheonette, several bars and a drugstore. There was a big empty storefront where groups of elderly people were playing bingo. Carole had suggested he try one of two restaurants near Dartmouth, but he didn't want to get back in the car. He found a small pizzeria. Standing next to him at the counter was a sexy dark-haired man in his twenties, a little shorter and heavier than Jonathan, with blue eyes and a five o'clock shadow. Maybe he was the baby's dad! Life suddenly seemed complicated. Jonathan wasn't sure he was ready.

The man took his slice and left. Jonathan sat in a booth near a window. The pizza was pretty good. He wished they served wine. Not many people walked by, but he looked for the Jewish gay neighbor who'd meant so much to Carole. No one seemed possible.

The next morning he picked Carole up at her apartment to drive her to Dr. Vo's office. Despite the cold, she was standing outside her small brick apartment building, her black ski jacket half-unzipped. When she got in and fastened her seatbelt, he couldn't help seeing how big her belly had gotten. He had the impulse to say something he would never say—Zowie!

During the half hour drive they made small talk. There were many awkward silences. At one point she said the baby was kicking and asked if he wanted to feel it.

"But I guess you're driving," she added quickly.

Not sure if he should pull over, he kept driving.

Dr. Vo's practice was associated with Dartmouth Hospital. There were two other men in the waiting room. People must assume he was the dad. He wasn't sure if that was exactly true. Carole took out her phone. She was wearing a pink top with ruffles on the sleeves. It looked stretched out and faded. Maybe she bought it at the thrift shop where she worked. He checked to see if she still had rubber bands around her wrist. She did.

The waiting room had photographs of mountains and lakes on the walls; the only reading material was about gynecology. One of the pregnant women reminded him of a colleague. He tried to think about a Larkin poem, but finally just sat there.

A nurse came in and announced that Dr. Vo had an emergency. She couldn't say how long the wait would be. Two of the pregnant women agreed to see the other physician. Soon Jonathan was the only "dad." After a while, only he and Carole were left.

Carole had put her phone away and was staring into space. Her hand was on her stomach. Idly, Jonathan asked her if she'd thought any more about going back to school.

"As I said, I'd be happy to help with applications."

"Okay," she said. "You offered already. Enough!"

They barely knew each other, and he'd managed to make her angry.

"There's a Yiddish word, genug—it means 'enough,'"

he said quickly. "My mom—she's been dead ten years now—she'd use all these Yiddish expressions." He smiled at Carole.

She didn't smile back.

"Anyway, she'd tell this story about when I was a little boy."

He used to hate it when she did.

"One day I got angry with her about something, and I happened to be holding a pencil. And, I threw it at her." Why was he telling this stupid story?

"It didn't hit her or anything. Actually she caught it, but then she kept going on about how it could have hit her. 'See how sharp that point is? It could have gone into my eye! You could have really hurt me.' She went on and on about it. Finally I said, 'Genug Mom.'" He smiled.

"Were you a bad boy?" Carole asked.

The idea seemed to please her.

"I guess. Sometimes."

She took out her phone.

"Listen, can I ask you a question?" He didn't wait for her answer. "I've noticed you wear these rubber bands." He gestured toward her wrist. "I'm wondering, is there something special you use them for?"

She smiled. "Lots of things. Like they make the lids of jars easier to grip. You can wrap a rubber band around the end of a candle, so when you put it in the candleholder it'll be less wobbly. You can shorten an electrical cord with a rubber band. Maybe this is TMI, but before I got maternity pants, I used a rubber band to keep my jeans closed."

The nurse told Carole she could go in. Jonathan would join her later.

He texted Peter that he was about to hear the baby's heartbeat.

When the nurse called him in, Carole, in a green robe, was lying down. Dr. Vo, Asian, petite and pretty, was fiddling with some equipment.

"This is Jonathan," Carole said. "I told you about him. He's a professor at a college in New York."

Dr. Vo nodded but barely glanced at him.

"He lives in Manhattan."

Jonathan wished for Carole's sake that Dr. Vo would at least pretend to be a little interested in him. He felt like saying something like, She's just as good as you are.

Apparently there was a problem with the baby's heartbeat or with hearing the baby's heartbeat.

"It doesn't necessarily mean anything at all," Dr. Vo said. She went to get a different machine.

Jonathan wasn't sure what to do. "Do you want me to wait outside?" he asked Carole.

"No. I don't know. I guess so." Maybe it was the green gown, but she looked sort of green.

Walking out, he realized he should have offered again to stay. And now here he was in an empty waiting room, alone again.

After a few minutes the nurse came to the doorway.

"Everything's fine," she said. "But Dr. Vo had another emergency. You'll have to hear baby's heart another time."

He was close to tears. "The important thing is the baby."

He wanted to buy Carole lunch at the nicest restaurant around, but she said she was wiped out and just wanted to go home and take a nap.

As she suggested, after he dropped her off he drove

back to Hanover, had lunch at a fancy hotel and walked around the Dartmouth campus. He and Carole had planned to have an early dinner, but she called and said she still wasn't up to being with anyone.

He told himself that he had no right to be, but he was hurt. He could have gone to her apartment and made her dinner. It had been a long time since he'd cooked for anyone.

He ate pizza at the same place. It wasn't as good.

He was surprised the next morning when Carole called from the lobby.

"I was afraid you checked out. Can I come up?"

He threw some clothes in his suitcase. As she knocked he was throwing the spread over the bed he'd slept in.

"Come in!" he said heartily. "Excuse the mess."

She kept on her unzipped jacket.

He took his suitcase off the chair, but she didn't sit down.

"I meant to ask you, did you like Dr. Vo?"

"Very much."

"She also teaches medical students," she said proudly. "At Dartmouth."

"Really good school." He wondered what she wanted.

"Listen, remember when you asked me what I do with my rubber bands? Give me one of your dress shirts. I'll show you how to pack it."

"Now? I mean, unfortunately I only brought this one…" he looked down at his shirt, "and the ones I already wore."

"That's okay."

He went to his suitcase and reluctantly handed her a wrinkled shirt.

Ignoring the other two beds, she spread it out on the rumpled one he'd slept in.

"Watch carefully," she said.

First she buttoned it. She turned it over, folded the sleeves in some way he doubted he'd remember, folded the shirt length-wise and then rolled it up from the bottom. She took a rubber band off her wrist and put it around the middle of the shirt.

"Packing it this way keeps it from wrinkling." She handed it to him.

"Great! That's great!" He put it in his suitcase.

"Do you have a book with you?" she asked him.

"I just brought my Kindle."

She took another rubber band from her wrist and gave it to him.

"When you get home, you can use this as a bookmark."

Carefully he put it in his wallet.

If she ever had a child that she…he couldn't think of a better word than "kept"…she probably knew about lots of rubber band projects they could do together. Their apartment would look like a cheery nursery school classroom. For the first time, he felt sorry for her, giving up her child.

Three weeks before the baby was due Carole didn't respond to either his text asking how things were going or to his email, and she didn't answer his text the next day asking if everything was all right. He went from being sure something terrible had happened to her or to the baby to worrying she'd changed her mind about the adoption. Maybe the dad had reached out and she'd taken him back. Or a gay couple was suddenly in the picture, and she'd decided that two dads were better than one.

Too nervous to do it himself, Jonathan asked Peter to call her local police and hospital. Nothing.

At night he lay awake. He should have found a bigger apartment. He should have joined a temple. He could have done a lot of things. He felt as if someone had died.

Whenever he went out he'd notice children everywhere. A toddler in his building was often in the lobby with his nanny, and he kept saying bye-bye to Jonathan.

"Bye-bye," Jonathan would croon. Then he'd turn around and say it again. And then again.

The third day Carole called.

"There's something I have to tell you."

She was crying, and at first he couldn't understand what she was saying.

At Carole's check-up, a new nurse had inadvertently revealed the baby's sex.

"At first I was so upset, I couldn't do anything. But I'm better now. And don't worry. I'm not going to tell you. Unless you really want to know." She paused. "Do you want to know the sex?"

"I'm fine."

He didn't say that he was so relieved, he didn't give a fuck about the gender.

Carole went into labor on a sunny morning in early May. Jonathan's bag had been packed for weeks, each shirt neatly folded and rolled up with a rubber band. He got to the hospital that evening, and a few days later he took his baby home.

Thank You

My fellow writers: Walter Cummins, Aurora Ferrero, Bill Glass, Andrey Henkin, and Nancy Novick.

Carolyn Waters and the New York Society Library.

Sheena Gillespie, colleague and friend.

Rose Pastore, a new friend.

My son-in-law, Nick Gaffney.

My husband, Jim.

And many thanks to my children, Emma and Jacob.

Karen Wunsch has published stories and essays in *Epoch, The Literary Review, Columbia Journal,* the *Michigan Quarterly Review,* and other journals. She taught writing and literature at Queensborough Community College. She lives in New York City.

www.ingramcontent.com/pod-product-compliance
Lightning Source LLC
Chambersburg PA
CBHW050357190726
48284CB00007BB/2326